MARK TWAIN.
TOM SAWYER

STERLING CHILDREN'S BOOKS
New York

An Imprint of Sterling Publishing Co., Inc.
1166 Avenue of the Americas
New York, NY 10036

STERLING CHILDREN'S BOOKS
AND THE DISTINCTIVE STERLING CHILDREN'S BOOKS
LOGO ARE REGISTERED TRADEMARKS
OF STERLING PUBLISHING CO., INC.

ISBN 978-1-4549-3814-9

DISTRIBUTED IN CANADA BY STERLING PUBLISHING CO., INC.
C/O CANADIAN MANDA GROUP, 664 ANNETTE STREET
TORONTO, ONTARIO M6S 2C8, CANADA
DISTRIBUTED IN THE UNITED KINGDOM BY GMC DISTRIBUTION SERVICES
CASTLE PLACE, 166 HIGH STREET, LEWES, EAST SUSSEX BN7 1XU, ENGLAND
DISTRIBUTED IN AUSTRALIA BY NEWSOUTH BOOKS,
UNIVERSITY OF NEW SOUTH WALES SYDNEY, NSW 2052, AUSTRALIA

FOR INFORMATION ABOUT CUSTOM EDITIONS,
SPECIAL SALES, AND PREMIUM AND CORPORATE PURCHASES,
PLEASE CONTACT STERLING SPECIAL SALES AT 800-805-5489
OR SPECIALSALES@STERLINGPUBLISHING.COM.

MANUFACTURED IN SINGAPORE
LOT #:
2   4   6   8   10   9   7   5   3   1
12/19

STERLINGPUBLISHING.COM

MARK TWAIN. TOM SAWYER

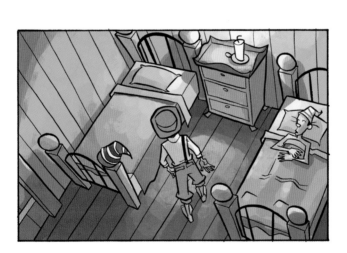

ADAPTED BY

TIM MUCCI
WRITER

RAD SECHRIST
ARTIST

STERLING CHILDREN'S BOOKS
New York

TO
ANDREA,
WHO SHOWS ME
EVERY DAY THAT
WE CAN BE WHO
WE WANT TO BE.

—T. M.

FOR MY ALWAYS
WONDERFUL
WIFE, MANDY.

—R. S.

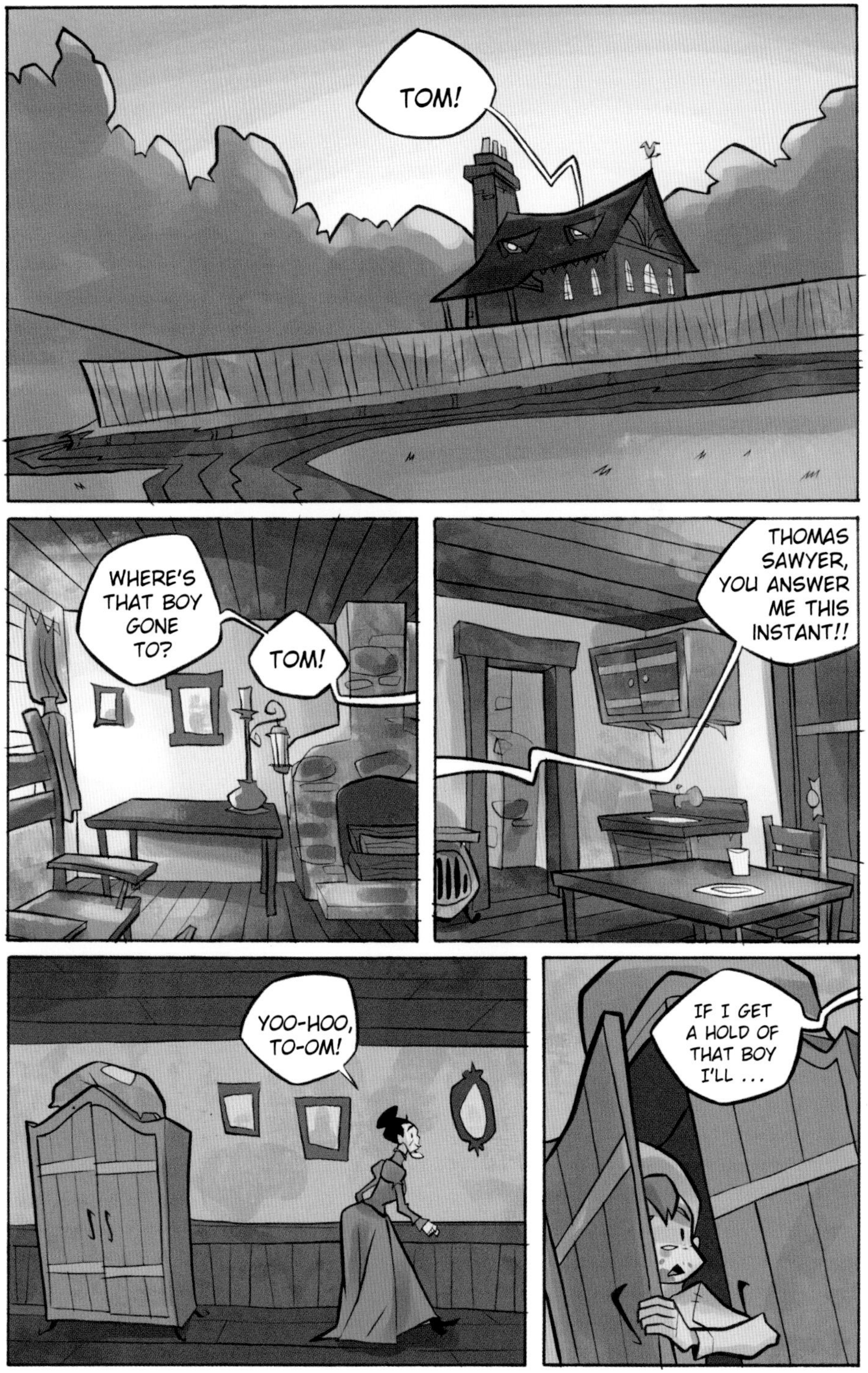
TOM!
WHERE'S THAT BOY GONE TO?
TOM!
THOMAS SAWYER, YOU ANSWER ME THIS INSTANT!!
YOO-HOO, TO-OM!
IF I GET A HOLD OF THAT BOY I'LL ...

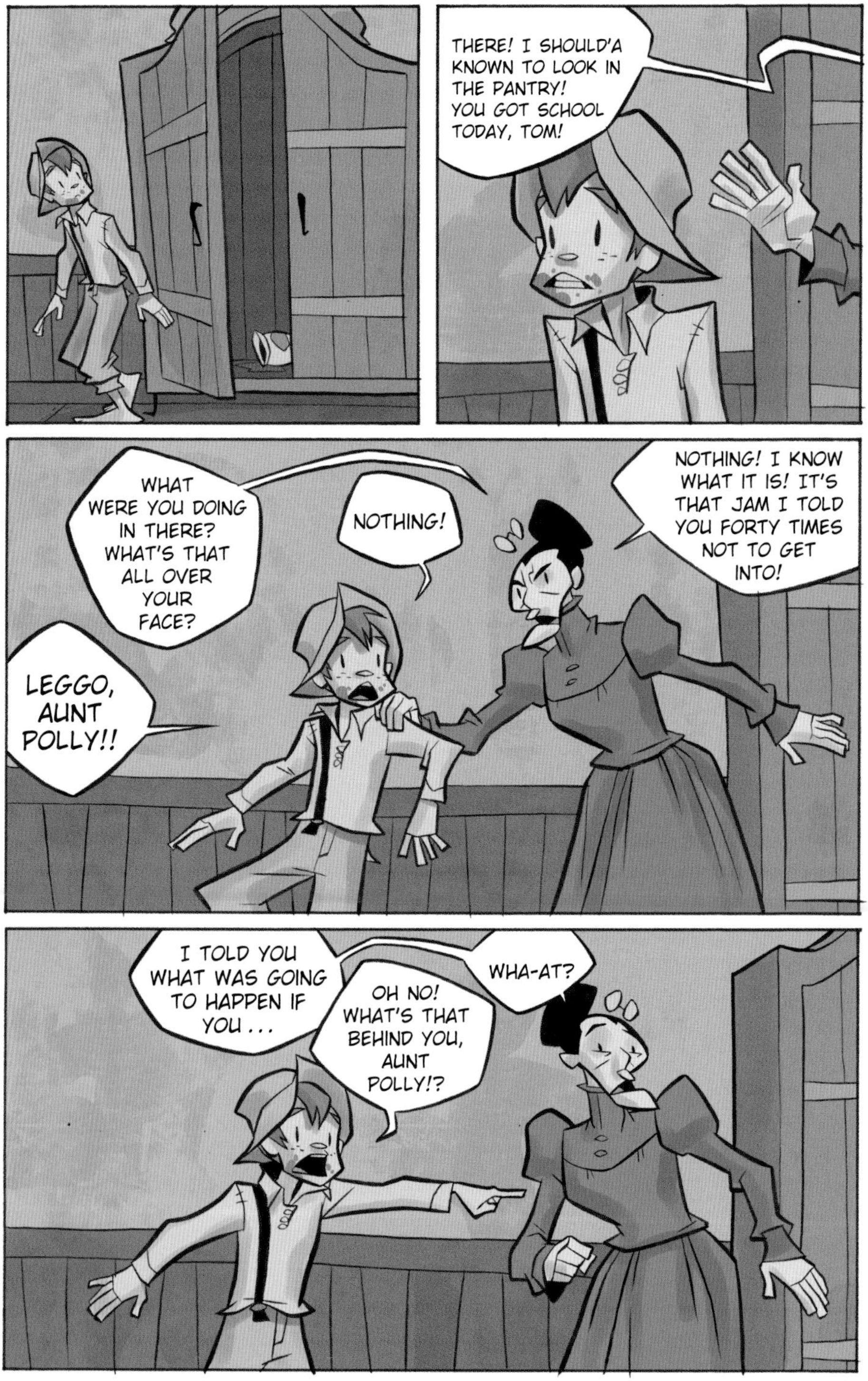
THERE! I SHOULD'A KNOWN TO LOOK IN THE PANTRY! YOU GOT SCHOOL TODAY, TOM!
WHAT WERE YOU DOING IN THERE? WHAT'S THAT ALL OVER YOUR FACE?
NOTHING!
NOTHING! I KNOW WHAT IT IS! IT'S THAT JAM I TOLD YOU FORTY TIMES NOT TO GET INTO!
LEGGO, AUNT POLLY!!
I TOLD YOU WHAT WAS GOING TO HAPPEN IF YOU . . .
OH NO! WHAT'S THAT BEHIND YOU, AUNT POLLY!?
WHA-AT?

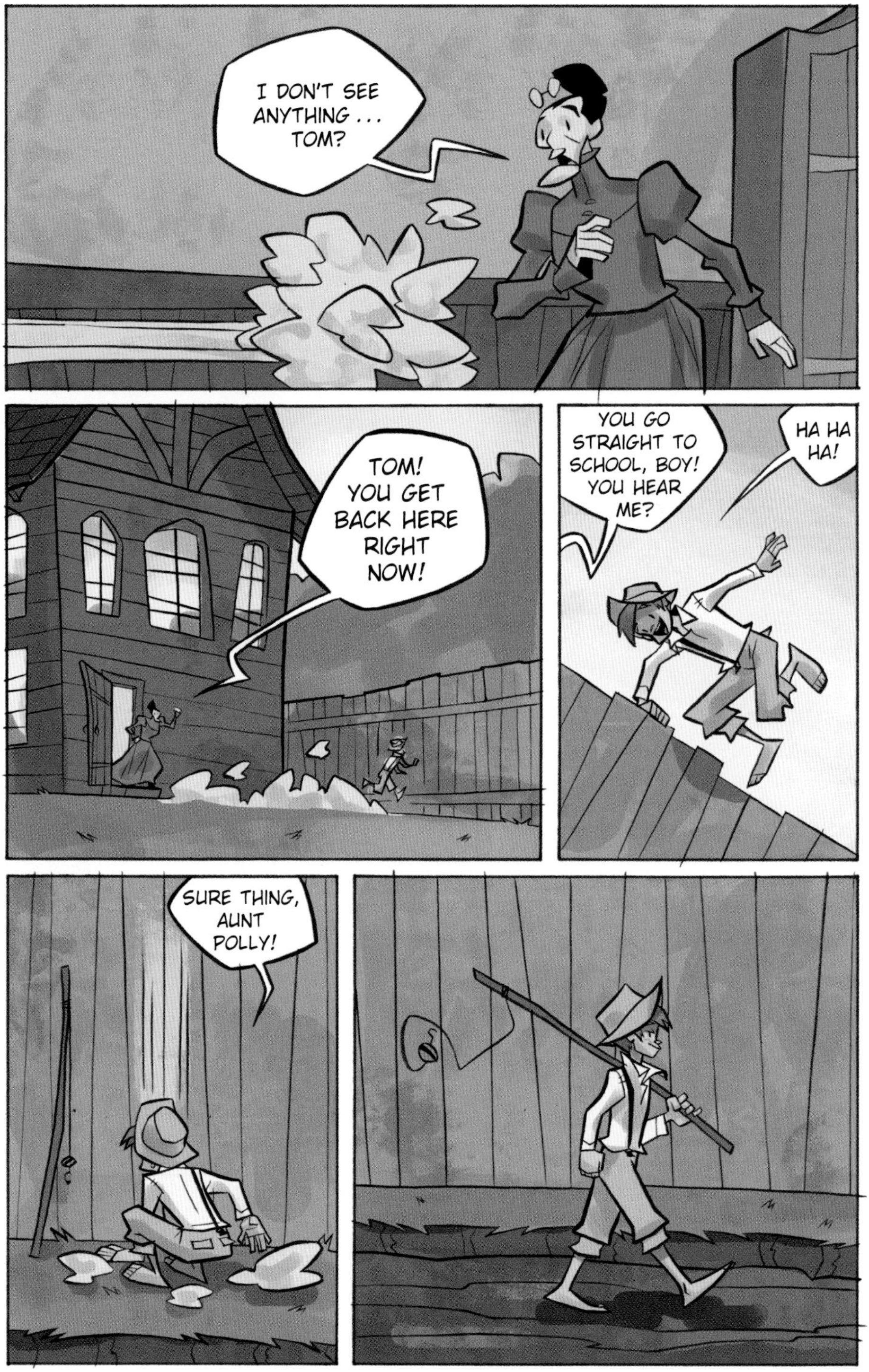
I DON'T SEE ANYTHING . . . TOM?
TOM! YOU GET BACK HERE RIGHT NOW!
YOU GO STRAIGHT TO SCHOOL, BOY! YOU HEAR ME?
HA HA HA!
SURE THING, AUNT POLLY!

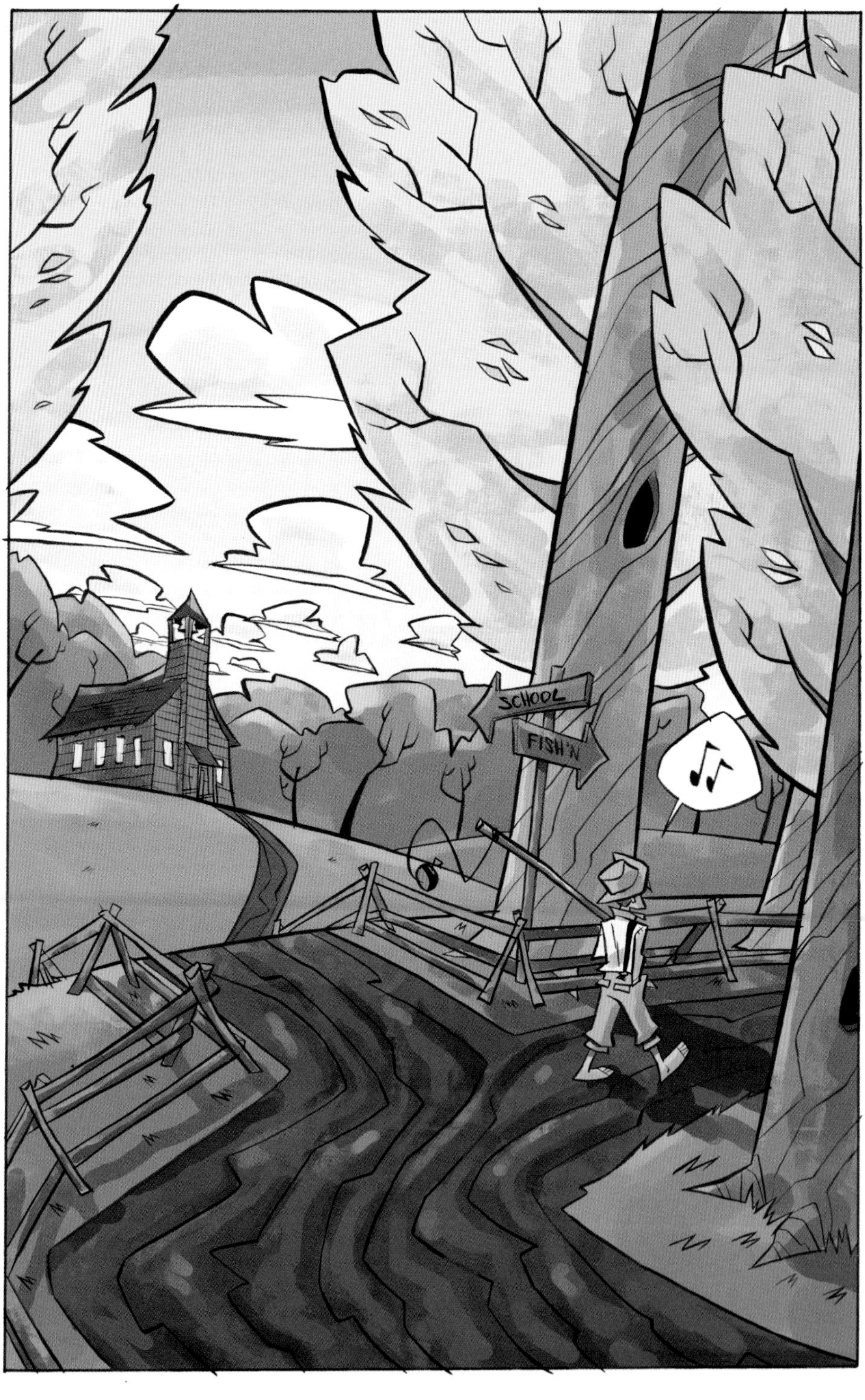
SCHOOL
FISH'N

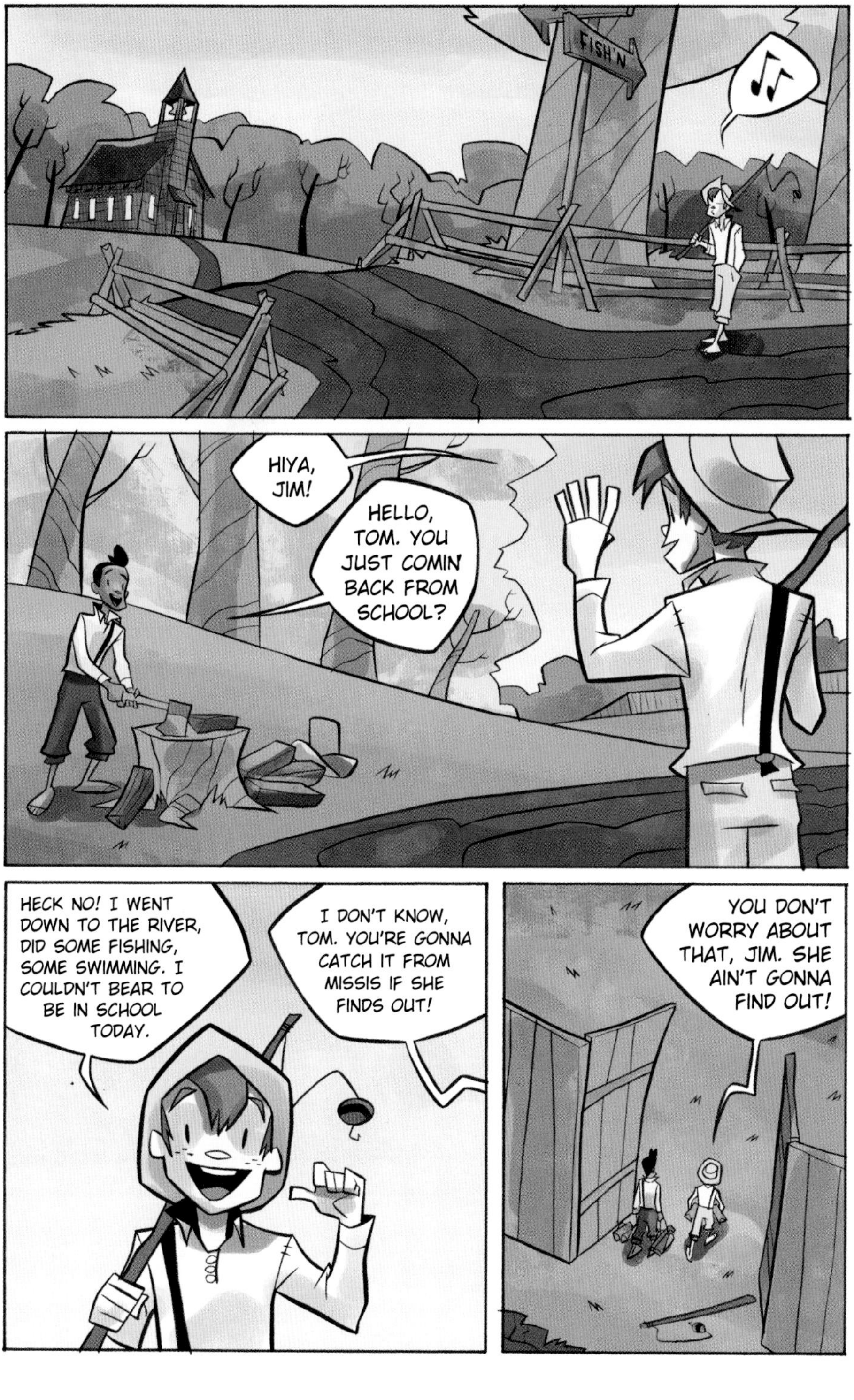
FISH'N
HIYA, JIM!
HELLO, TOM. YOU JUST COMIN' BACK FROM SCHOOL?
HECK NO! I WENT DOWN TO THE RIVER, DID SOME FISHING, SOME SWIMMING. I COULDN'T BEAR TO BE IN SCHOOL TODAY.
I DON'T KNOW, TOM. YOU'RE GONNA CATCH IT FROM MISSIS IF SHE FINDS OUT!
YOU DON'T WORRY ABOUT THAT, JIM. SHE AIN'T GONNA FIND OUT!

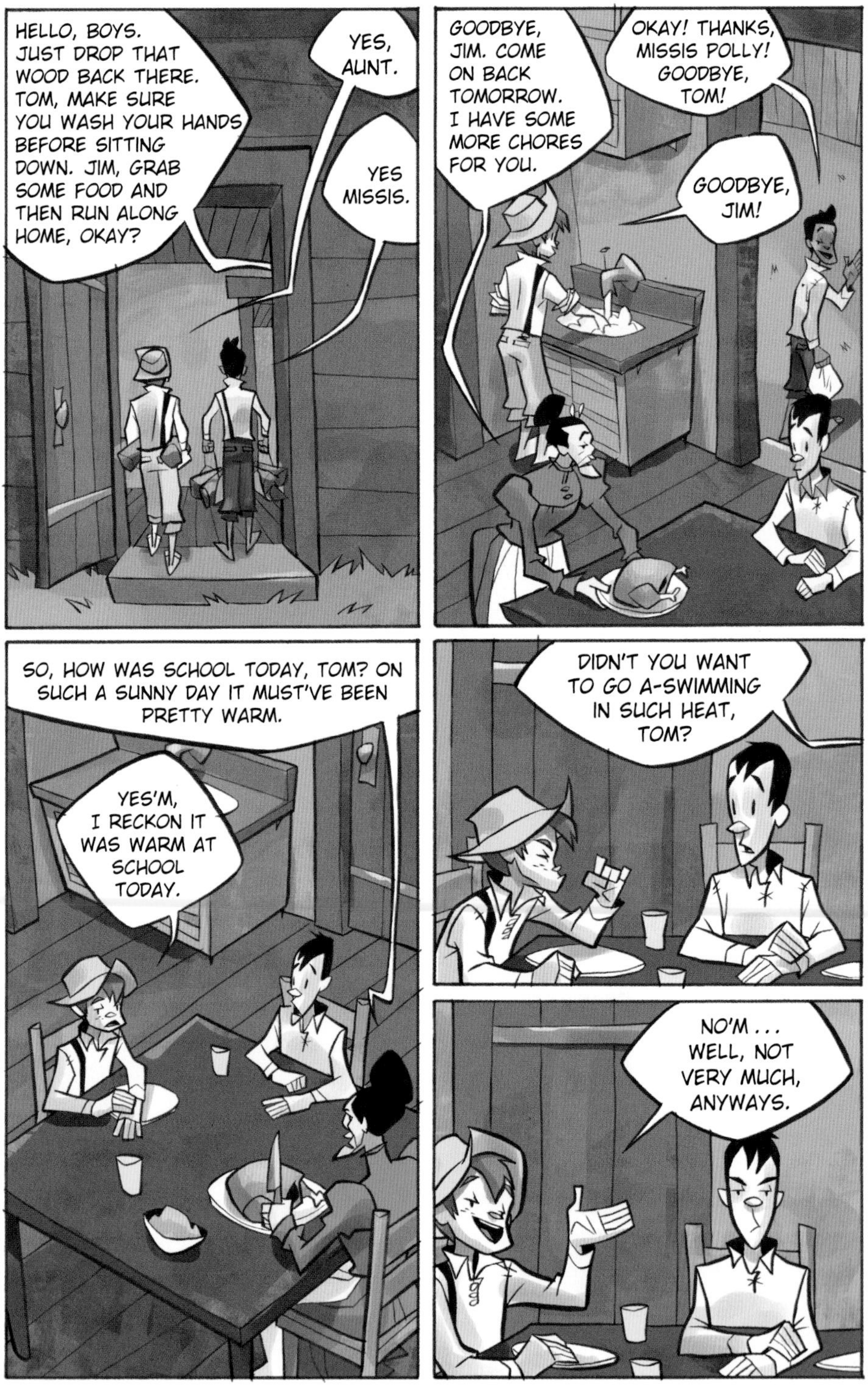
HELLO, BOYS. JUST DROP THAT WOOD BACK THERE. TOM, MAKE SURE YOU WASH YOUR HANDS BEFORE SITTING DOWN. JIM, GRAB SOME FOOD AND THEN RUN ALONG HOME, OKAY?
YES, AUNT.
YES MISSIS.
GOODBYE, JIM. COME ON BACK TOMORROW. I HAVE SOME MORE CHORES FOR YOU.
OKAY! THANKS, MISSIS POLLY! GOODBYE, TOM!
GOODBYE, JIM!
SO, HOW WAS SCHOOL TODAY, TOM? ON SUCH A SUNNY DAY IT MUST'VE BEEN PRETTY WARM.
YES'M, I RECKON IT WAS WARM AT SCHOOL TODAY.
DIDN'T YOU WANT TO GO A-SWIMMING IN SUCH HEAT, TOM?
NO'M . . . WELL, NOT VERY MUCH, ANYWAYS.

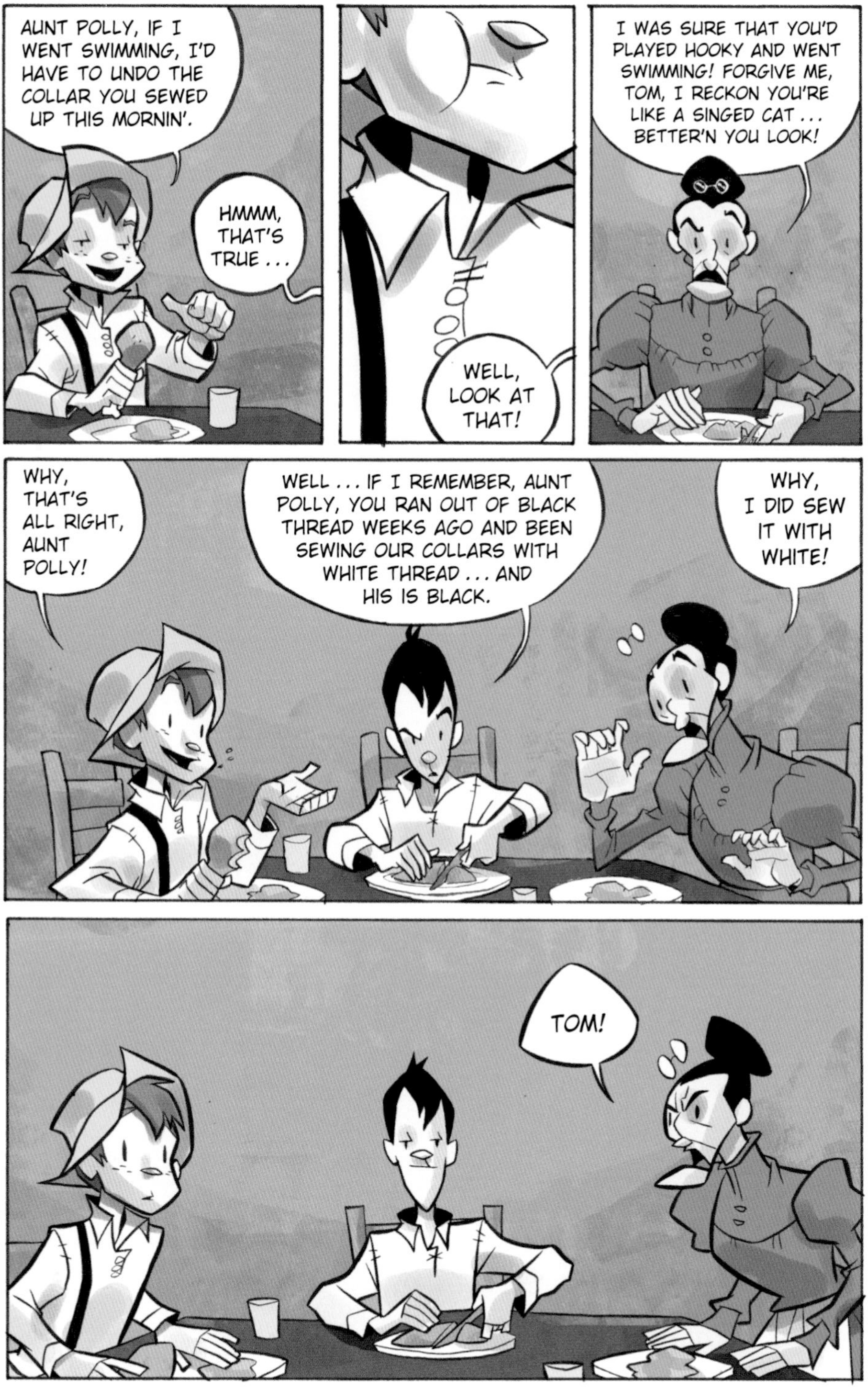
AUNT POLLY, IF I WENT SWIMMING, I'D HAVE TO UNDO THE COLLAR YOU SEWED UP THIS MORNIN'.
HMMM, THAT'S TRUE . . .
WELL, LOOK AT THAT!
I WAS SURE THAT YOU'D PLAYED HOOKY AND WENT SWIMMING! FORGIVE ME, TOM, I RECKON YOU'RE LIKE A SINGED CAT . . . BETTER'N YOU LOOK!
WHY, THAT'S ALL RIGHT, AUNT POLLY!
WELL . . . IF I REMEMBER, AUNT POLLY, YOU RAN OUT OF BLACK THREAD WEEKS AGO AND BEEN SEWING OUR COLLARS WITH WHITE THREAD . . . AND HIS IS BLACK.
WHY, I DID SEW IT WITH WHITE!
TOM!

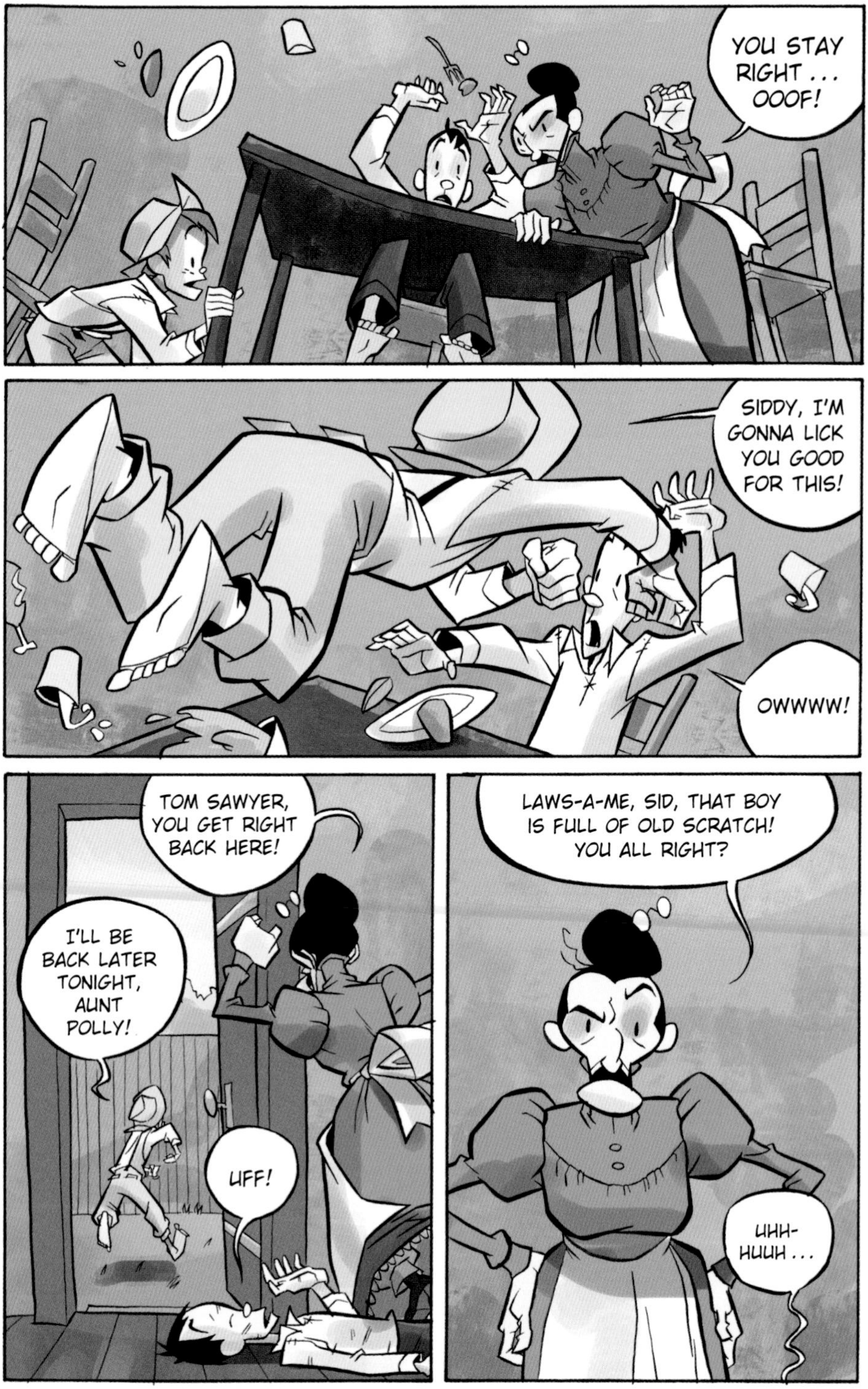
YOU STAY RIGHT . . . OOOF!
SIDDY, I'M GONNA LICK YOU GOOD FOR THIS!
OWWWW!
TOM SAWYER, YOU GET RIGHT BACK HERE!
I'LL BE BACK LATER TONIGHT, AUNT POLLY!
UFF!
LAWS-A-ME, SID, THAT BOY IS FULL OF OLD SCRATCH! YOU ALL RIGHT?
UHH-HUUH . . .

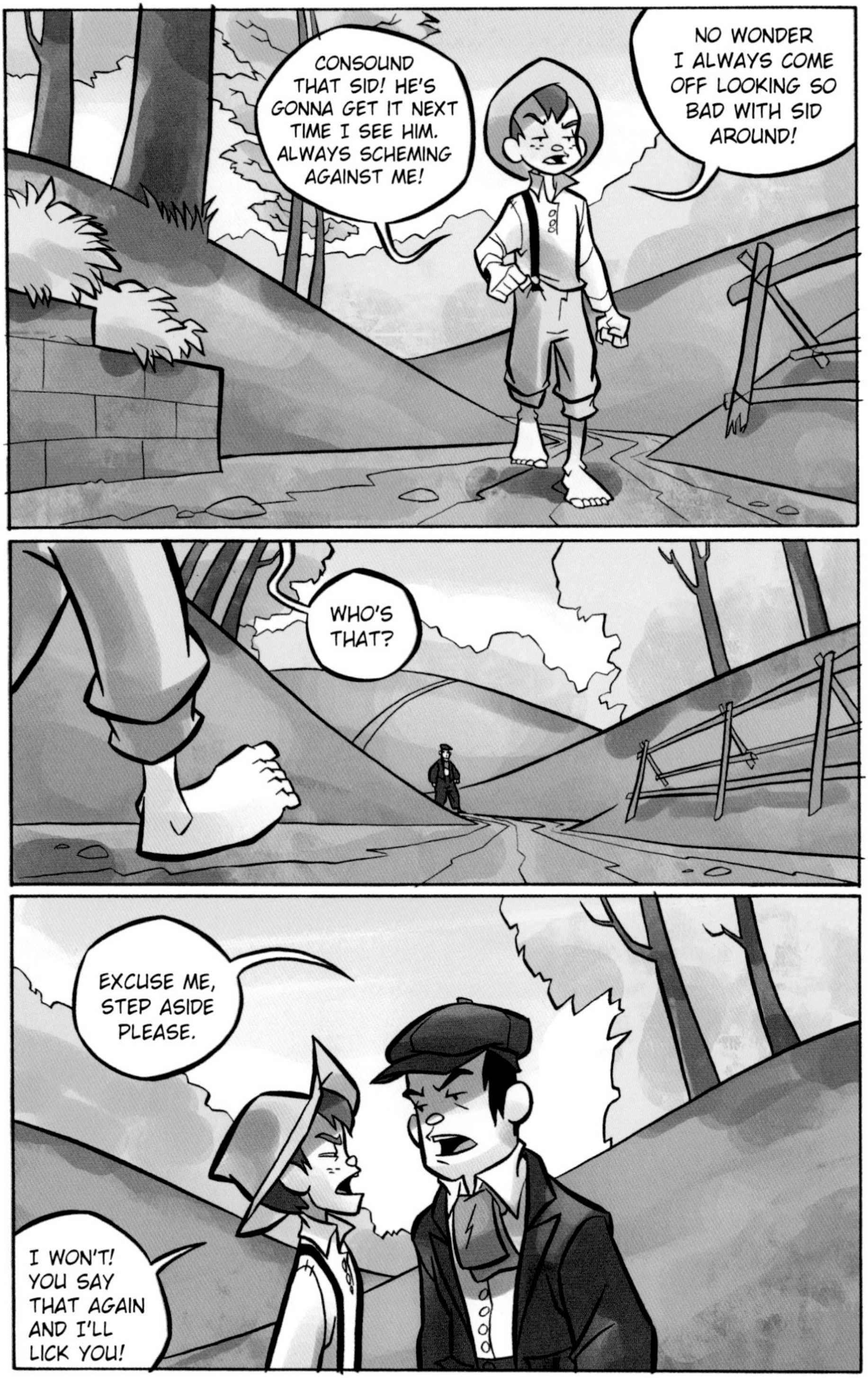
CONSOUND THAT SID! HE'S GONNA GET IT NEXT TIME I SEE HIM. ALWAYS SCHEMING AGAINST ME!
NO WONDER I ALWAYS COME OFF LOOKING SO BAD WITH SID AROUND!
WHO'S THAT?
EXCUSE ME, STEP ASIDE PLEASE.
I WON'T! YOU SAY THAT AGAIN AND I'LL LICK YOU!

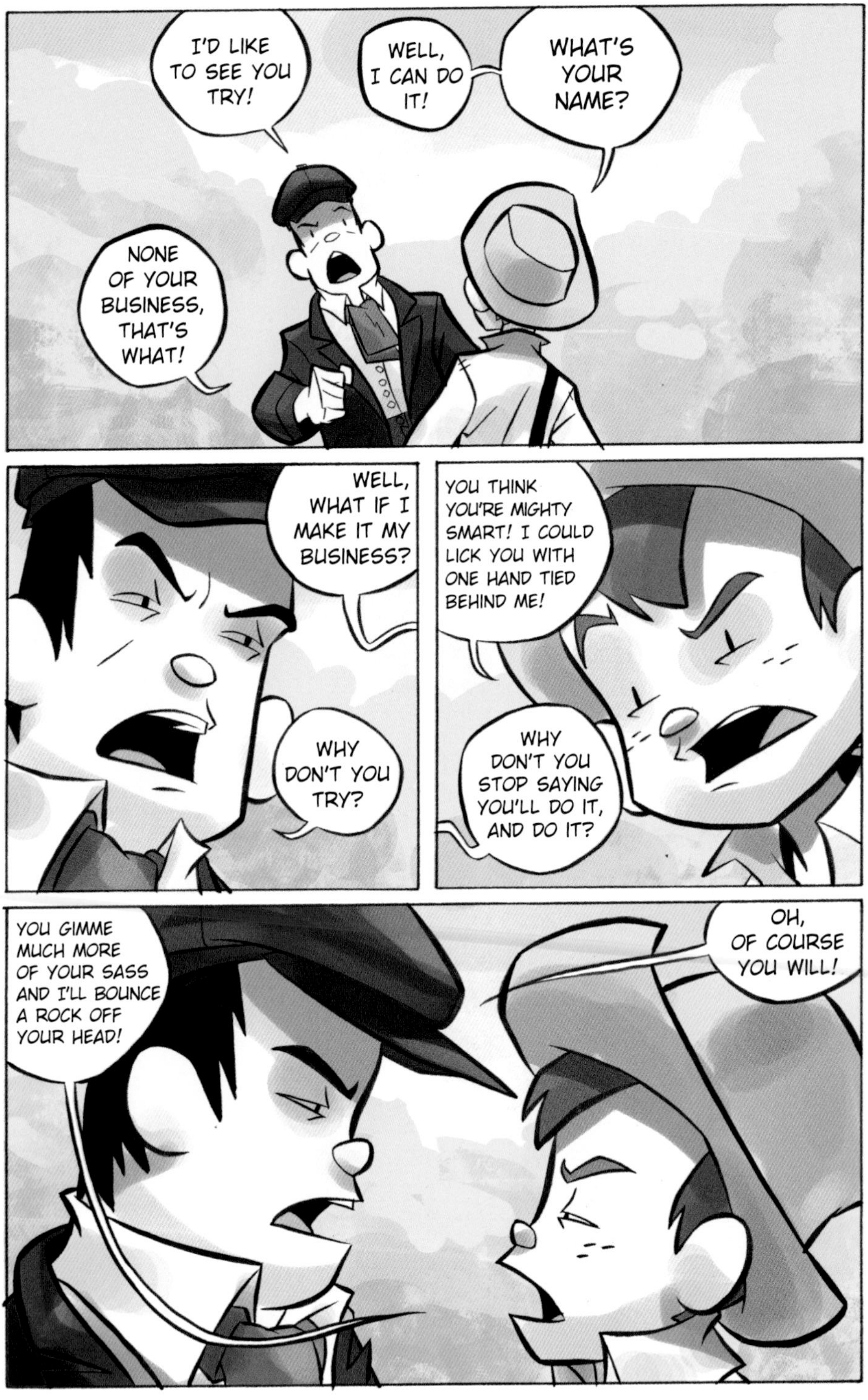
I'D LIKE TO SEE YOU TRY!
WELL, I CAN DO IT!
WHAT'S YOUR NAME?
NONE OF YOUR BUSINESS, THAT'S WHAT!
WELL, WHAT IF I MAKE IT MY BUSINESS?
WHY DON'T YOU TRY?
YOU THINK YOU'RE MIGHTY SMART! I COULD LICK YOU WITH ONE HAND TIED BEHIND ME!
WHY DON'T YOU STOP SAYING YOU'LL DO IT, AND DO IT?
YOU GIMME MUCH MORE OF YOUR SASS AND I'LL BOUNCE A ROCK OFF YOUR HEAD!
OH, OF COURSE YOU WILL!

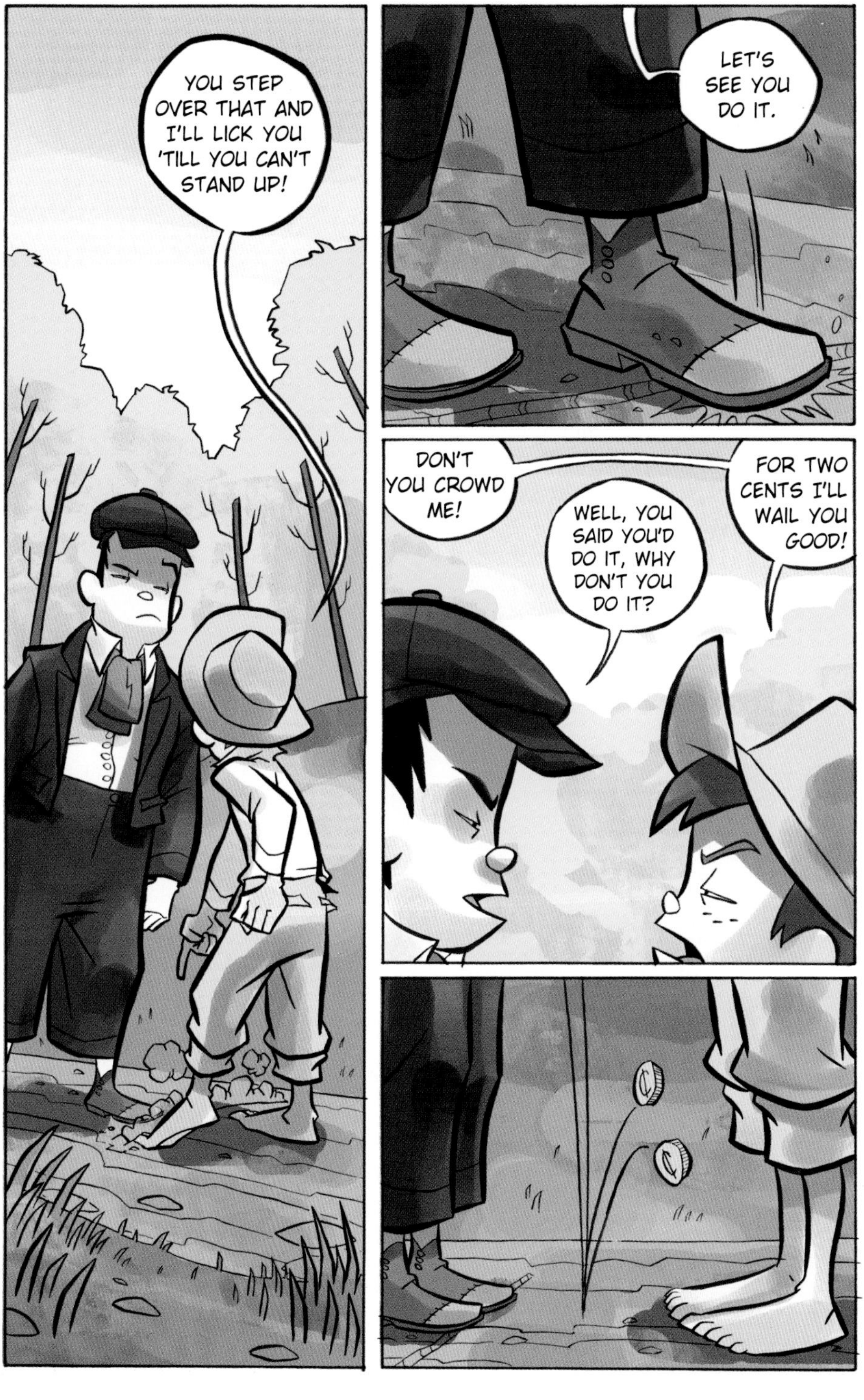
YOU STEP OVER THAT AND I'LL LICK YOU 'TILL YOU CAN'T STAND UP!
LET'S SEE YOU DO IT.
DON'T YOU CROWD ME!
FOR TWO CENTS I'LL WAIL YOU GOOD!
WELL, YOU SAID YOU'D DO IT, WHY DON'T YOU DO IT?

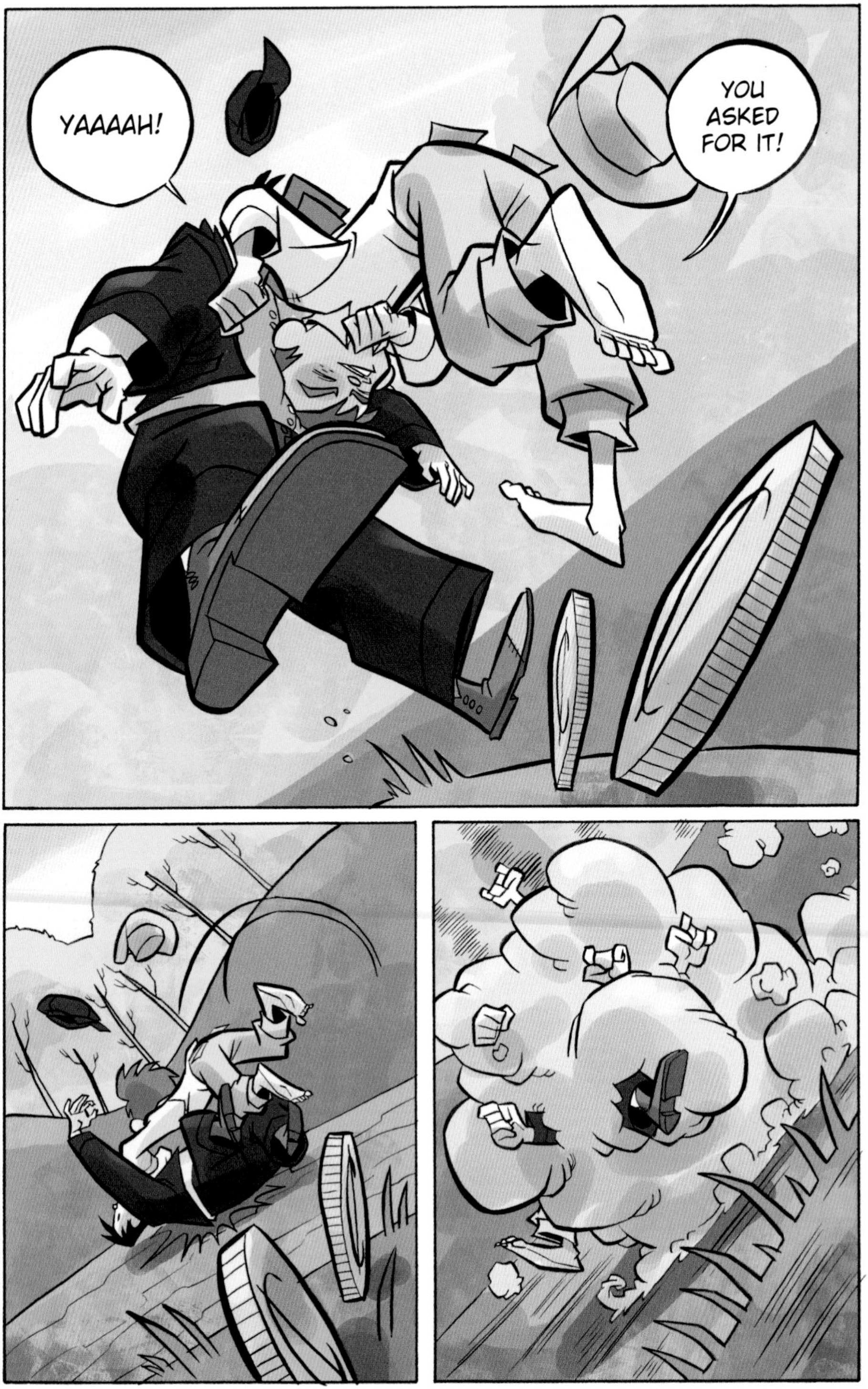
YAAAAH!
YOU ASKED FOR IT!

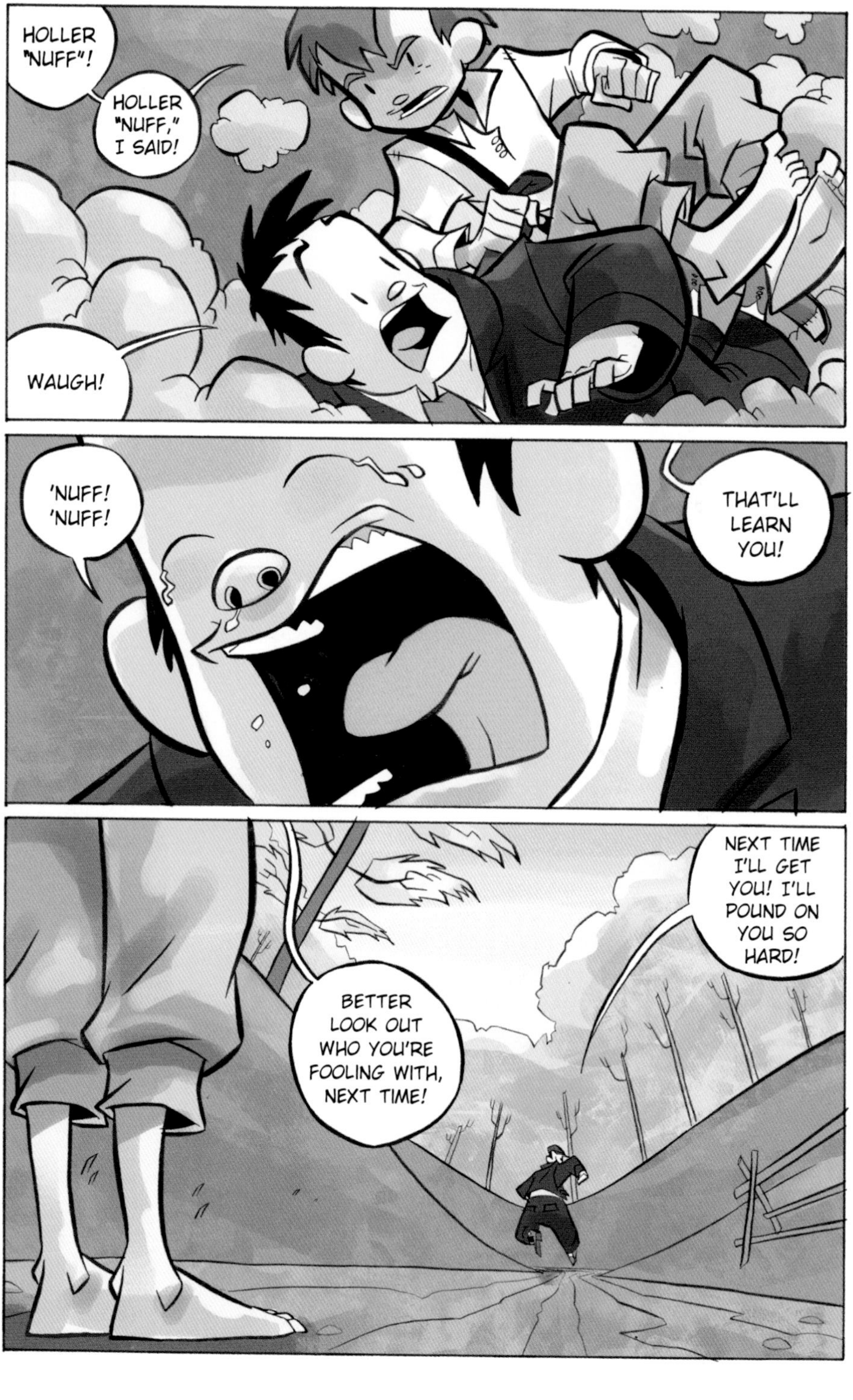
HOLLER "NUFF"!
HOLLER "NUFF," I SAID!
WAUGH!
'NUFF! 'NUFF!
THAT'LL LEARN YOU!
NEXT TIME I'LL GET YOU! I'LL POUND ON YOU SO HARD!
BETTER LOOK OUT WHO YOU'RE FOOLING WITH, NEXT TIME!

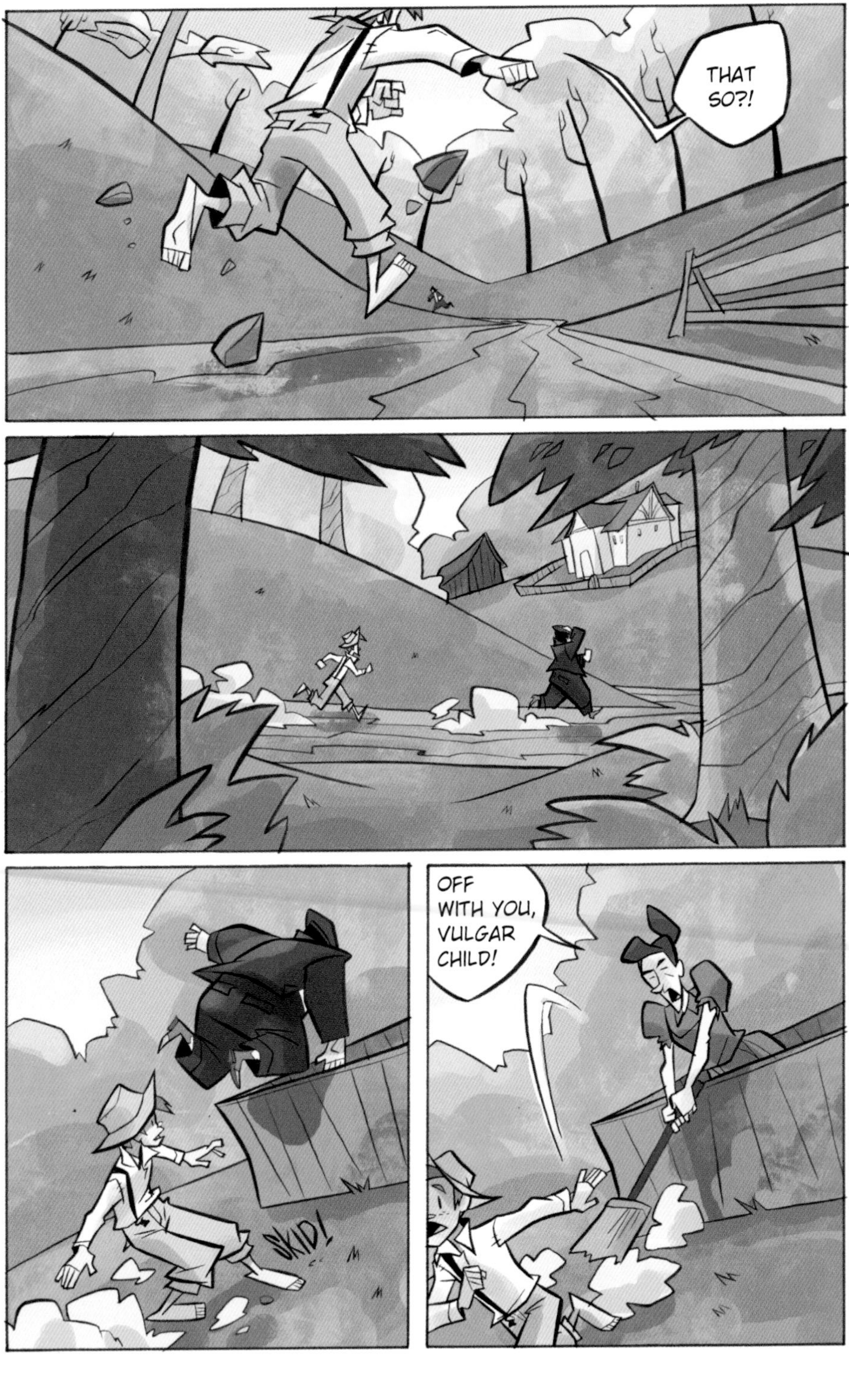
THAT SO?!
SKID!
OFF WITH YOU, VULGAR CHILD!

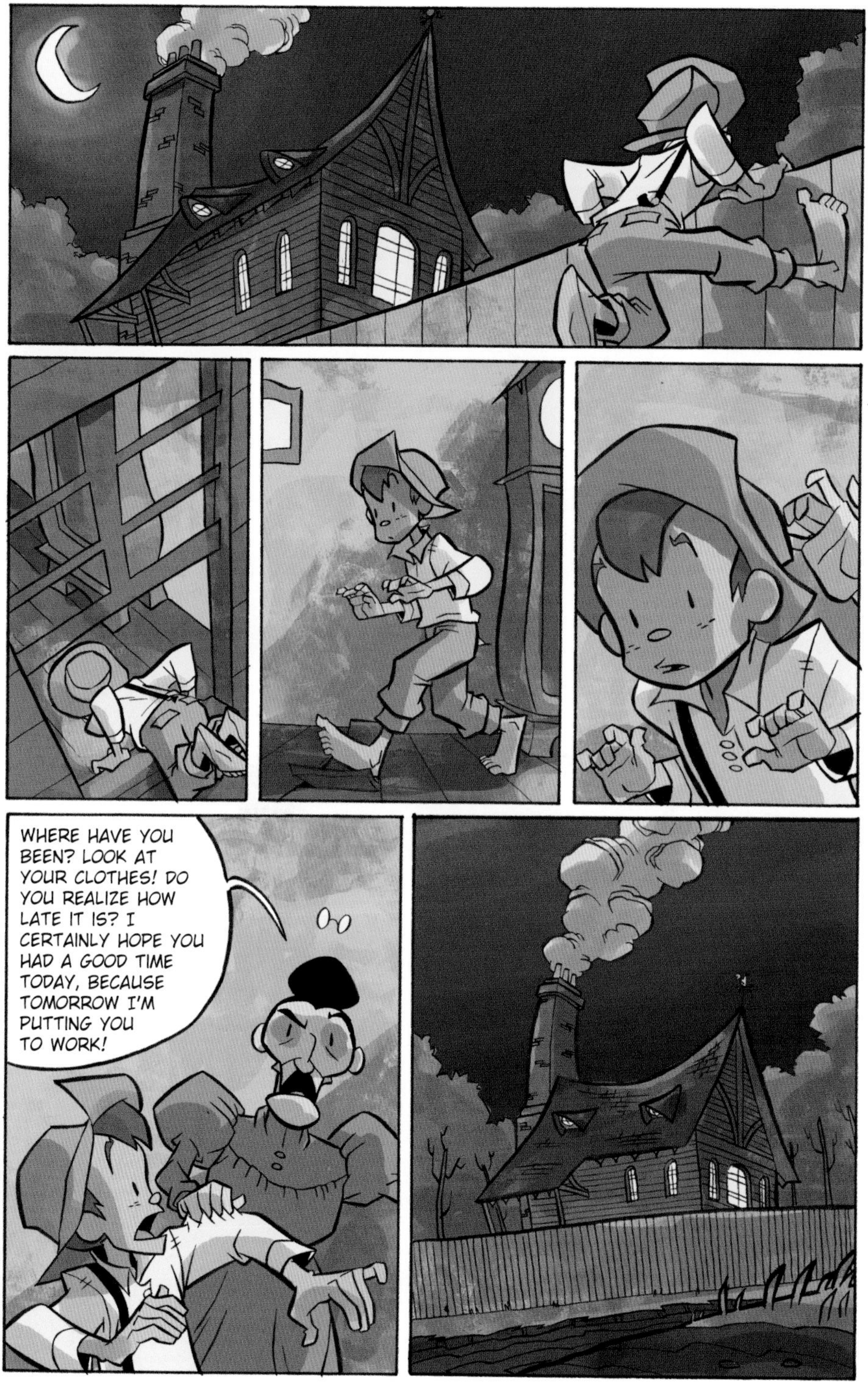
WHERE HAVE YOU BEEN? LOOK AT YOUR CLOTHES! DO YOU REALIZE HOW LATE IT IS? I CERTAINLY HOPE YOU HAD A GOOD TIME TODAY, BECAUSE TOMORROW I'M PUTTING YOU TO WORK!

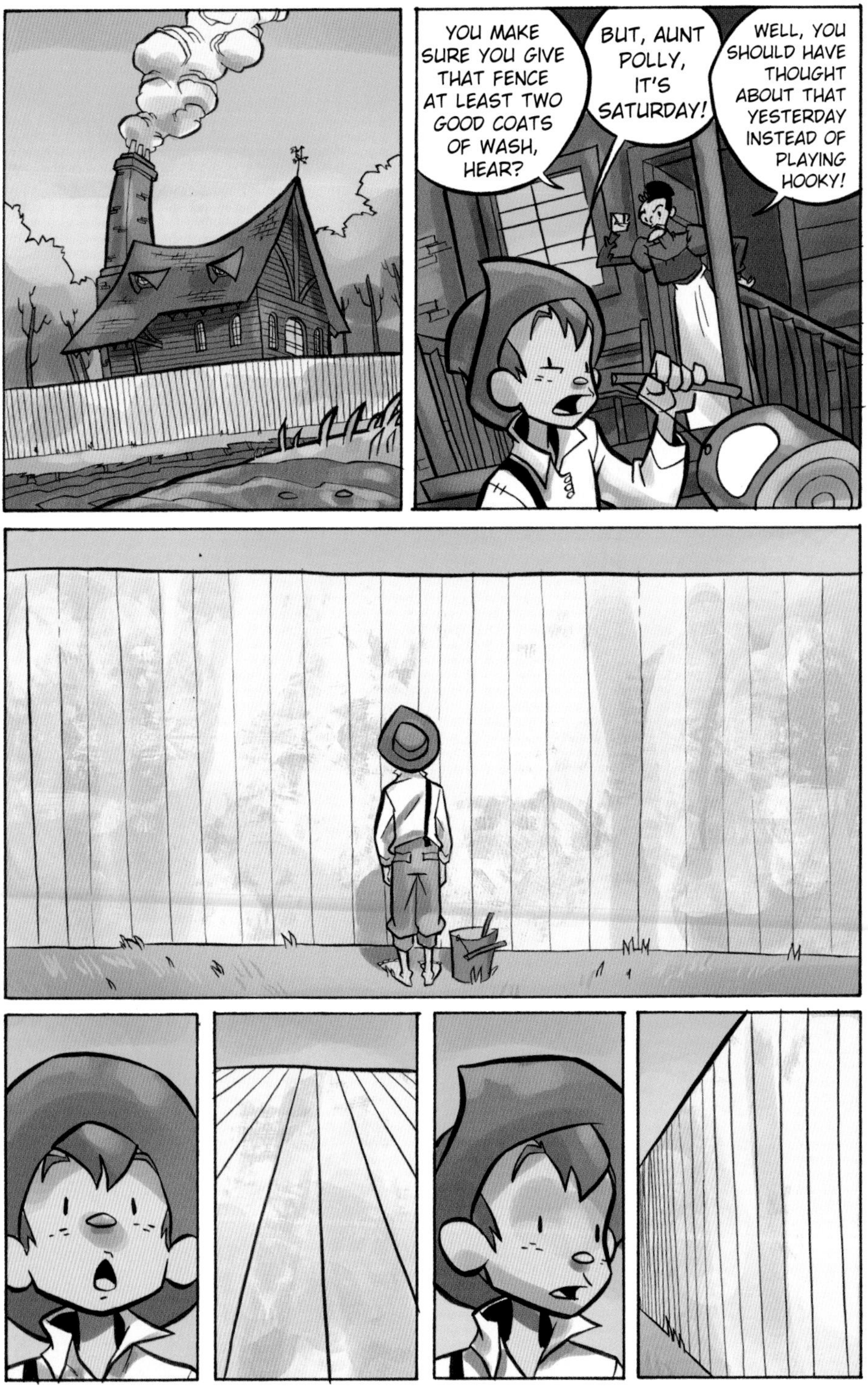
YOU MAKE SURE YOU GIVE THAT FENCE AT LEAST TWO GOOD COATS OF WASH, HEAR?
BUT, AUNT POLLY, IT'S SATURDAY!
WELL, YOU SHOULD HAVE THOUGHT ABOUT THAT YESTERDAY INSTEAD OF PLAYING HOOKY!

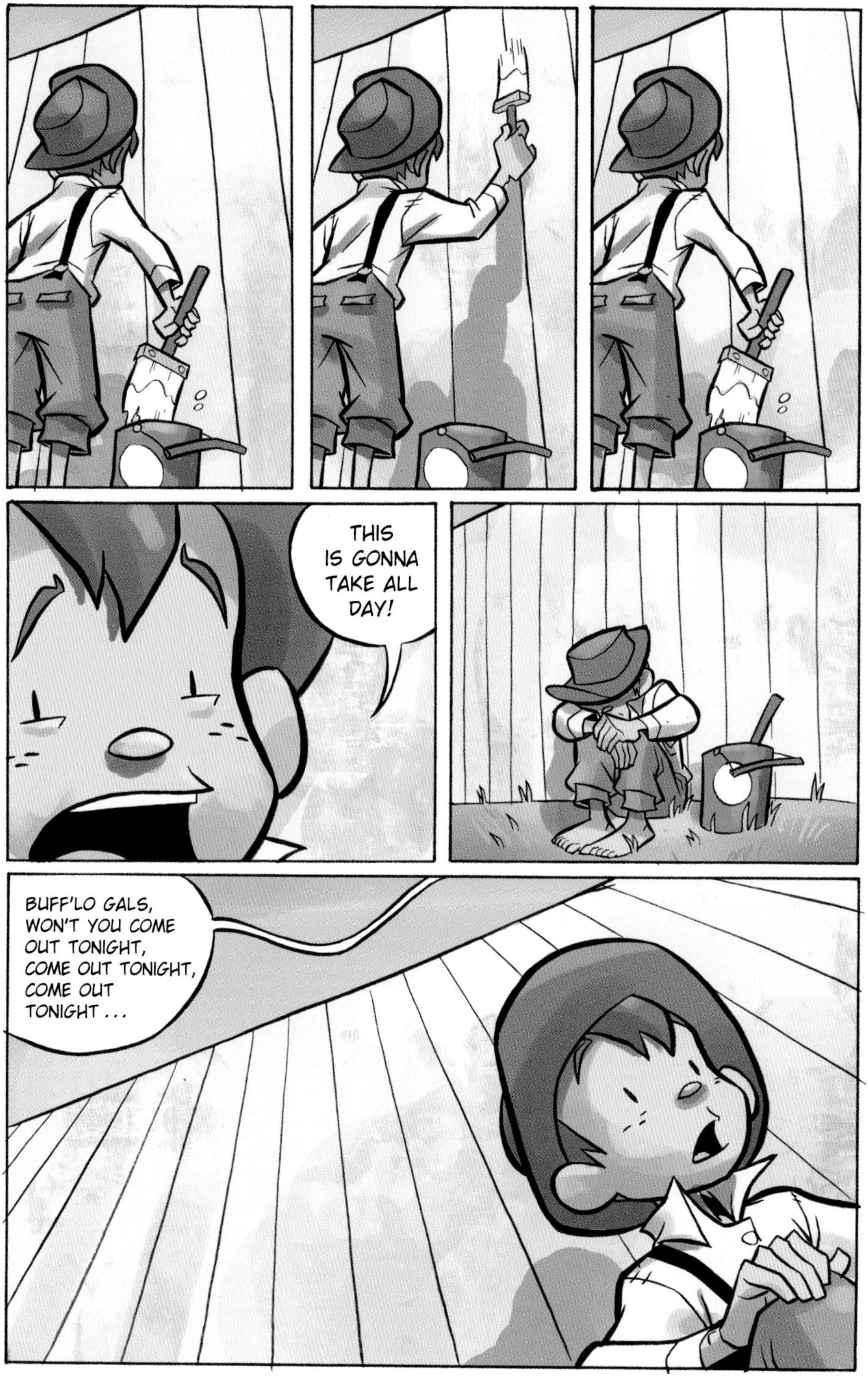
THIS IS GONNA TAKE ALL DAY!
BUFF'LO GALS, WON'T YOU COME OUT TONIGHT, COME OUT TONIGHT, COME OUT TONIGHT . . .

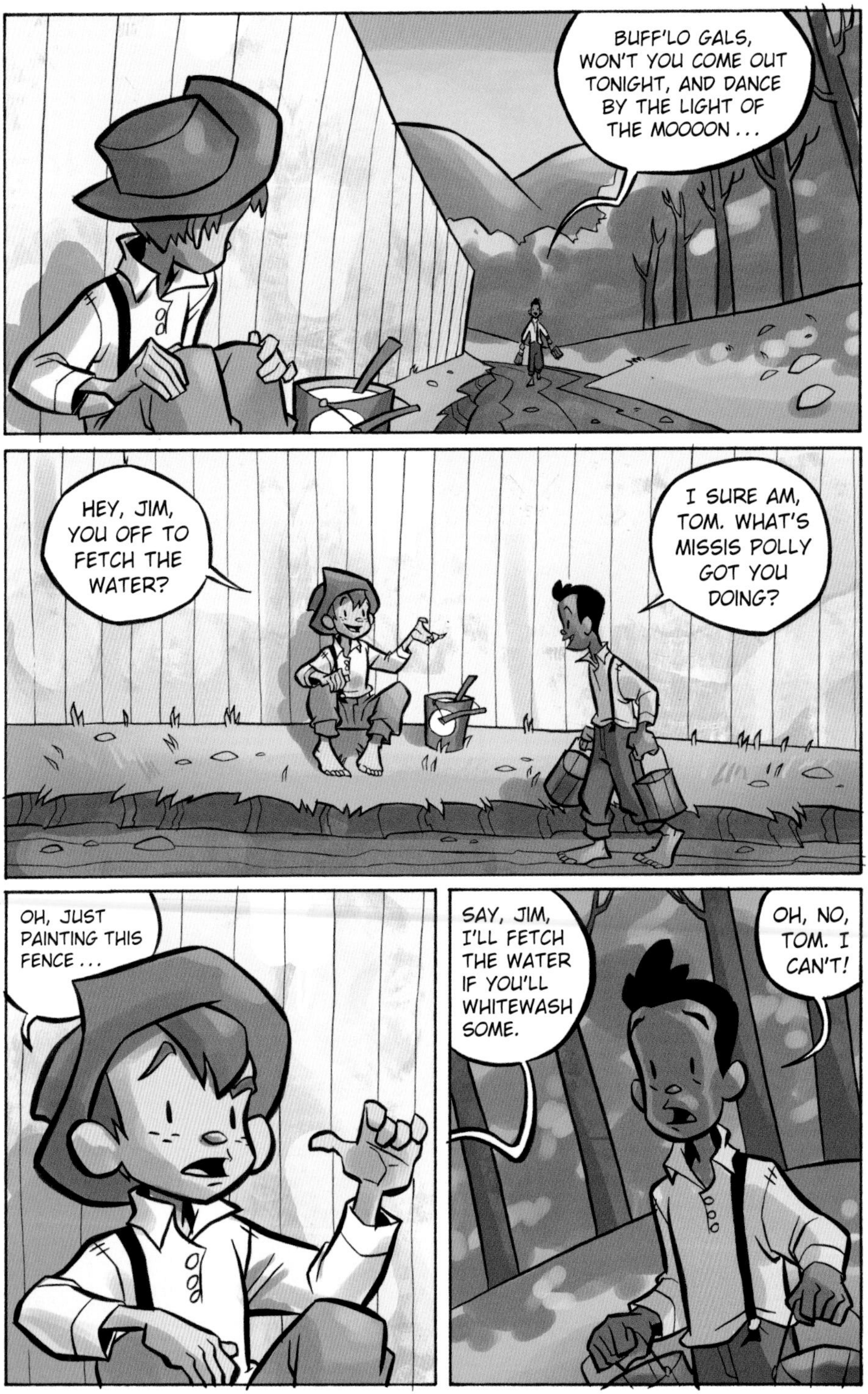
BUFF'LO GALS, WON'T YOU COME OUT TONIGHT, AND DANCE BY THE LIGHT OF THE MOOOON . . .
HEY, JIM, YOU OFF TO FETCH THE WATER?
I SURE AM, TOM. WHAT'S MISSIS POLLY GOT YOU DOING?
OH, JUST PAINTING THIS FENCE . . .
SAY, JIM, I'LL FETCH THE WATER IF YOU'LL WHITEWASH SOME.
OH, NO, TOM. I CAN'T!

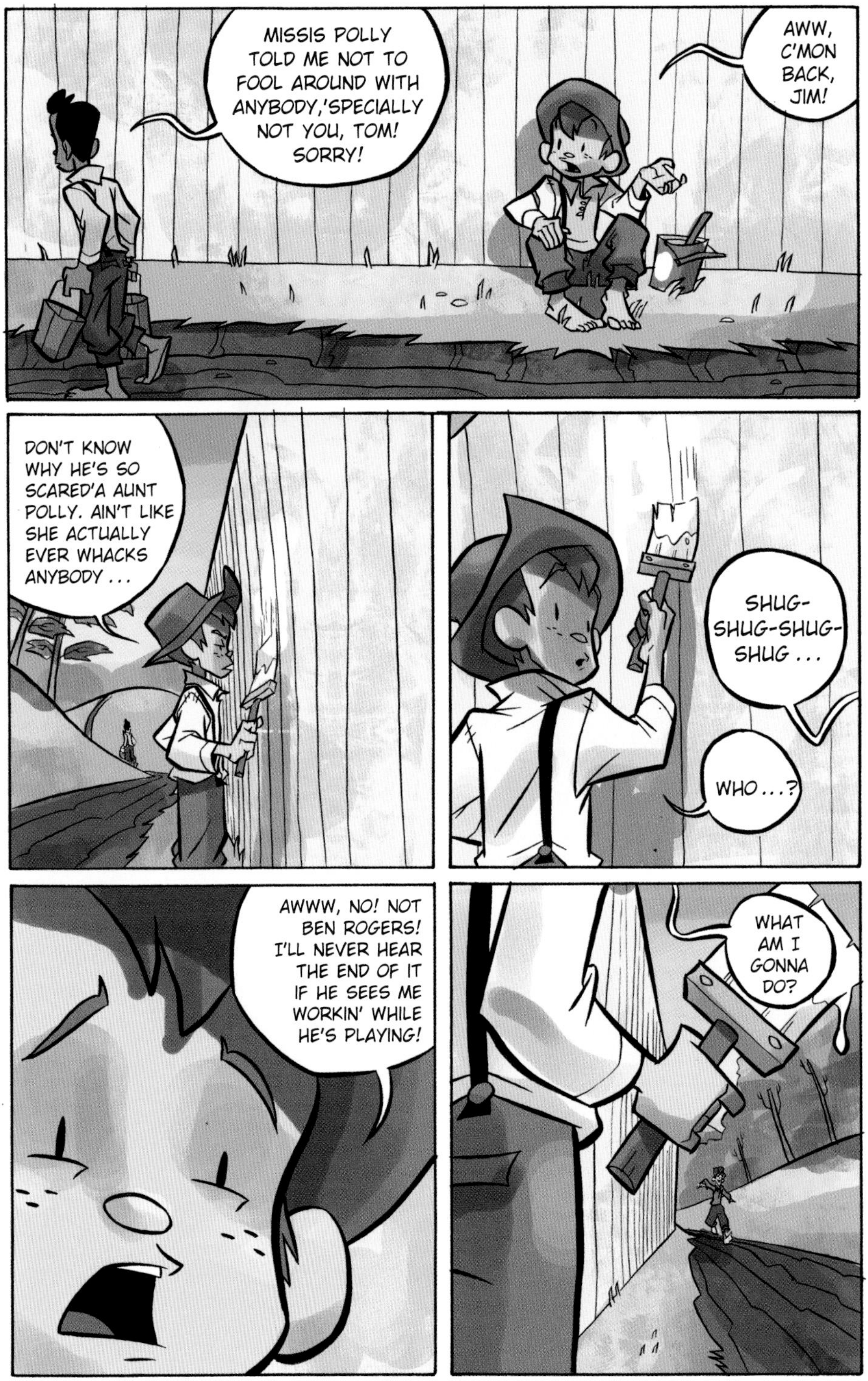
MISSIS POLLY TOLD ME NOT TO FOOL AROUND WITH ANYBODY,'SPECIALLY NOT YOU, TOM! SORRY!
AWW, C'MON BACK, JIM!
DON'T KNOW WHY HE'S SO SCARED'A AUNT POLLY. AIN'T LIKE SHE ACTUALLY EVER WHACKS ANYBODY . . .
SHUG-SHUG-SHUG-SHUG . . .
WHO . . .?
AWWW, NO! NOT BEN ROGERS! I'LL NEVER HEAR THE END OF IT IF HE SEES ME WORKIN' WHILE HE'S PLAYING!
WHAT AM I GONNA DO?

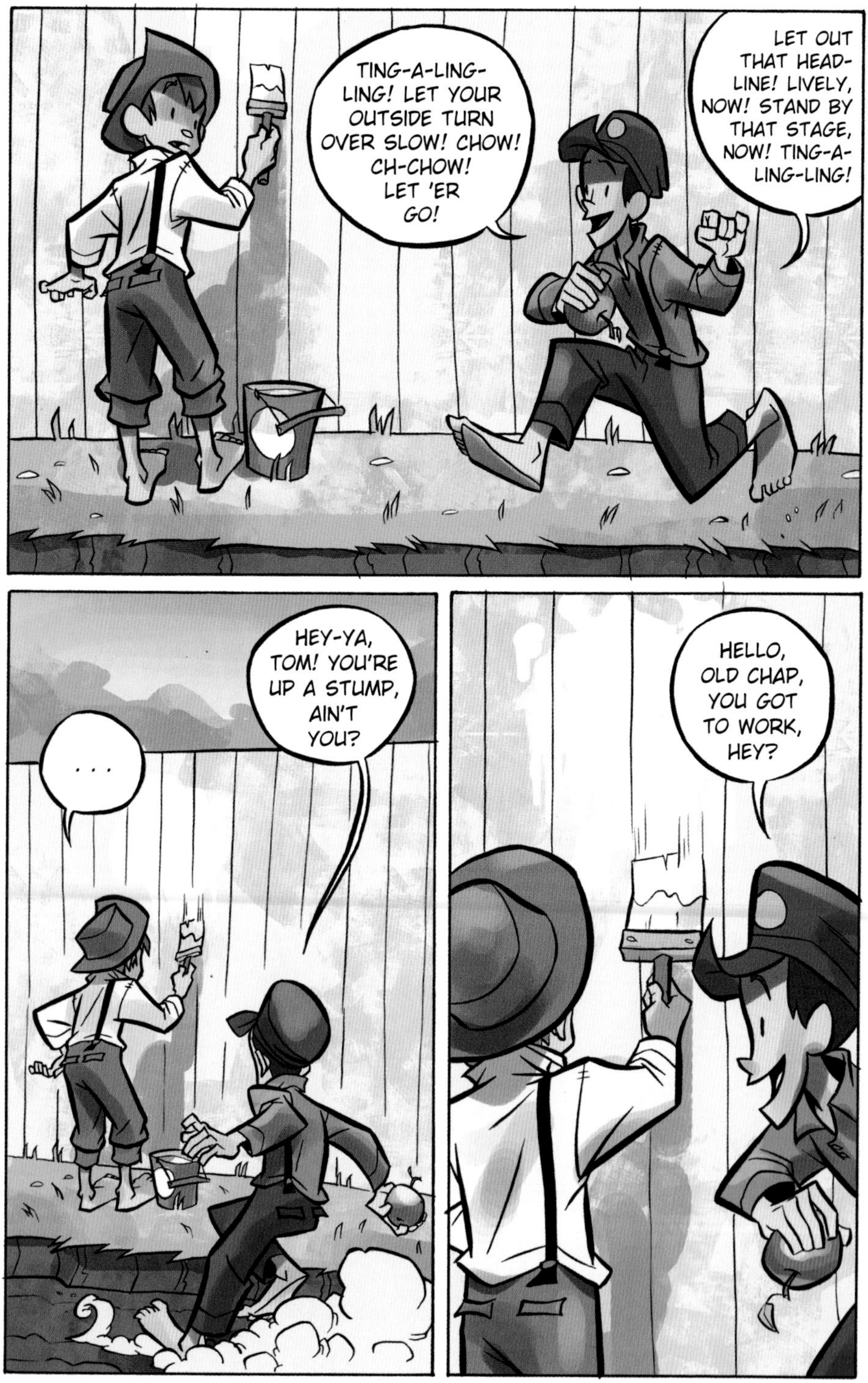
TING-A-LING-LING! LET YOUR OUTSIDE TURN OVER SLOW! CHOW! CH-CHOW! LET 'ER GO!
LET OUT THAT HEAD-LINE! LIVELY, NOW! STAND BY THAT STAGE, NOW! TING-A-LING-LING!
HEY-YA, TOM! YOU'RE UP A STUMP, AIN'T YOU?
. . .
HELLO, OLD CHAP, YOU GOT TO WORK, HEY?

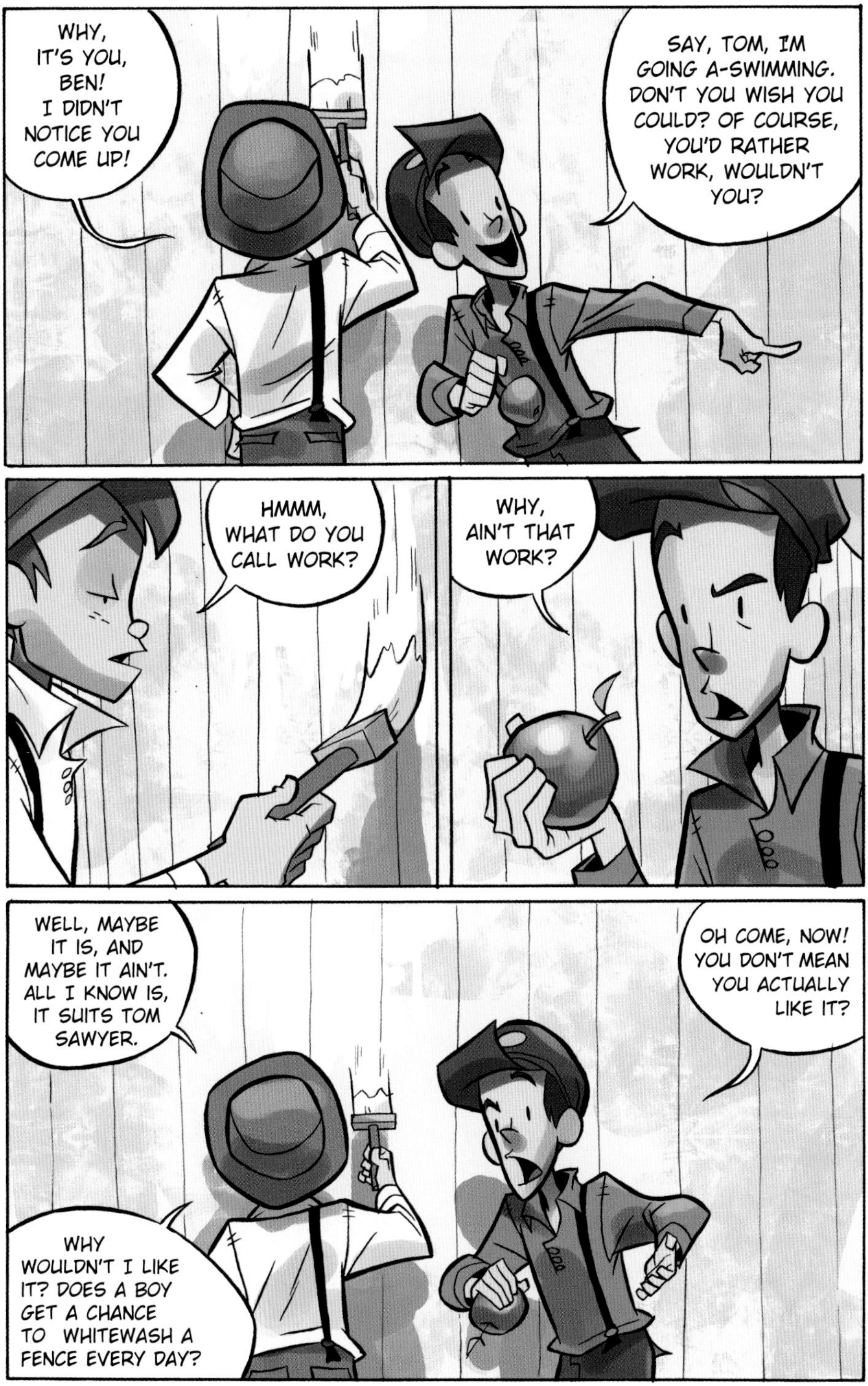
WHY, IT'S YOU, BEN! I DIDN'T NOTICE YOU COME UP!
SAY, TOM, I'M GOING A-SWIMMING. DON'T YOU WISH YOU COULD? OF COURSE, YOU'D RATHER WORK, WOULDN'T YOU?
HMMM, WHAT DO YOU CALL WORK?
WHY, AIN'T THAT WORK?
WELL, MAYBE IT IS, AND MAYBE IT AIN'T. ALL I KNOW IS, IT SUITS TOM SAWYER.
OH COME, NOW! YOU DON'T MEAN YOU ACTUALLY LIKE IT?
WHY WOULDN'T I LIKE IT? DOES A BOY GET A CHANCE TO WHITEWASH A FENCE EVERY DAY?

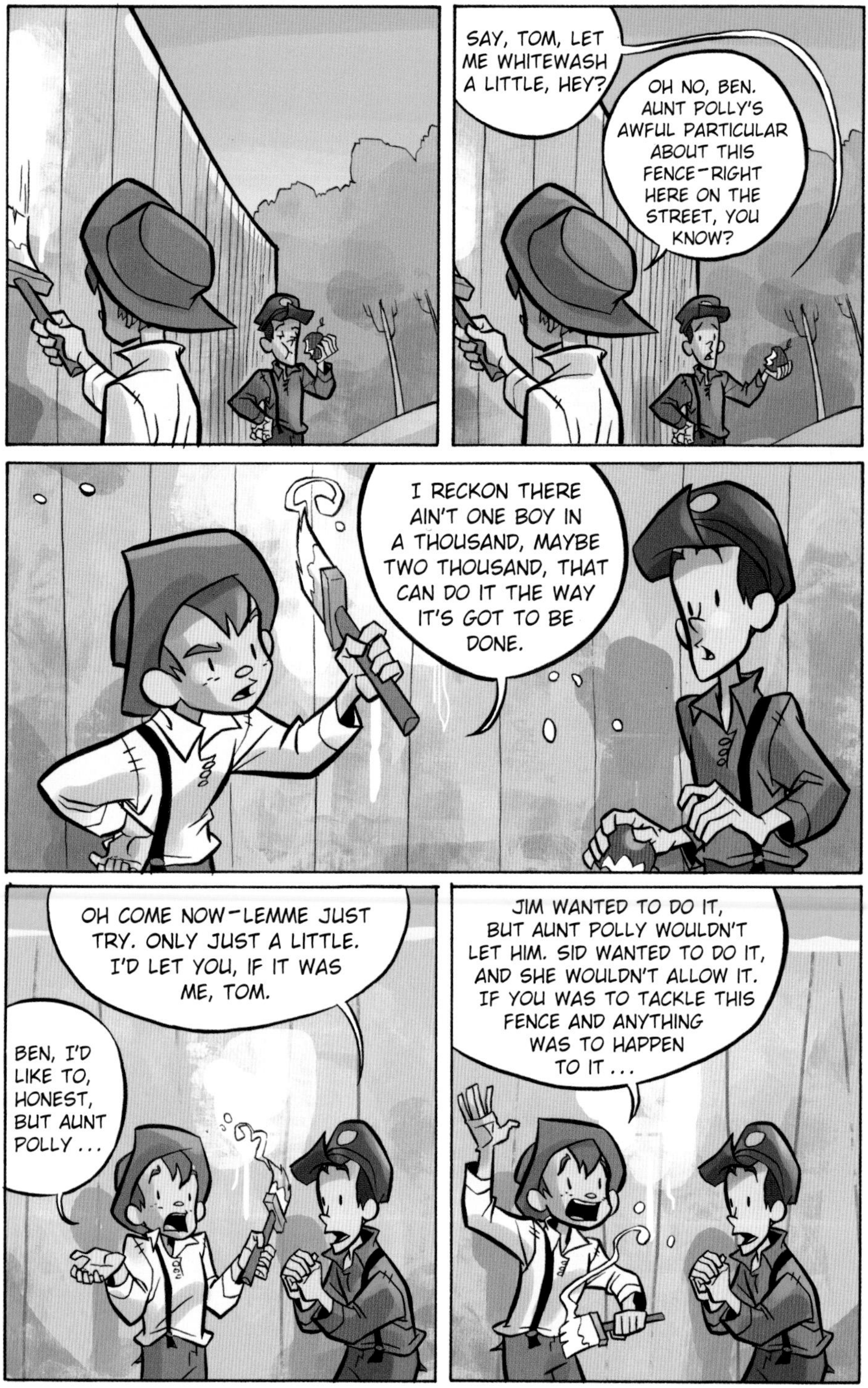
SAY, TOM, LET ME WHITEWASH A LITTLE, HEY?
OH NO, BEN. AUNT POLLY'S AWFUL PARTICULAR ABOUT THIS FENCE—RIGHT HERE ON THE STREET, YOU KNOW?
I RECKON THERE AIN'T ONE BOY IN A THOUSAND, MAYBE TWO THOUSAND, THAT CAN DO IT THE WAY IT'S GOT TO BE DONE.
OH COME NOW—LEMME JUST TRY. ONLY JUST A LITTLE. I'D LET YOU, IF IT WAS ME, TOM.
BEN, I'D LIKE TO, HONEST, BUT AUNT POLLY . . .
JIM WANTED TO DO IT, BUT AUNT POLLY WOULDN'T LET HIM. SID WANTED TO DO IT, AND SHE WOULDN'T ALLOW IT. IF YOU WAS TO TACKLE THIS FENCE AND ANYTHING WAS TO HAPPEN TO IT . . .

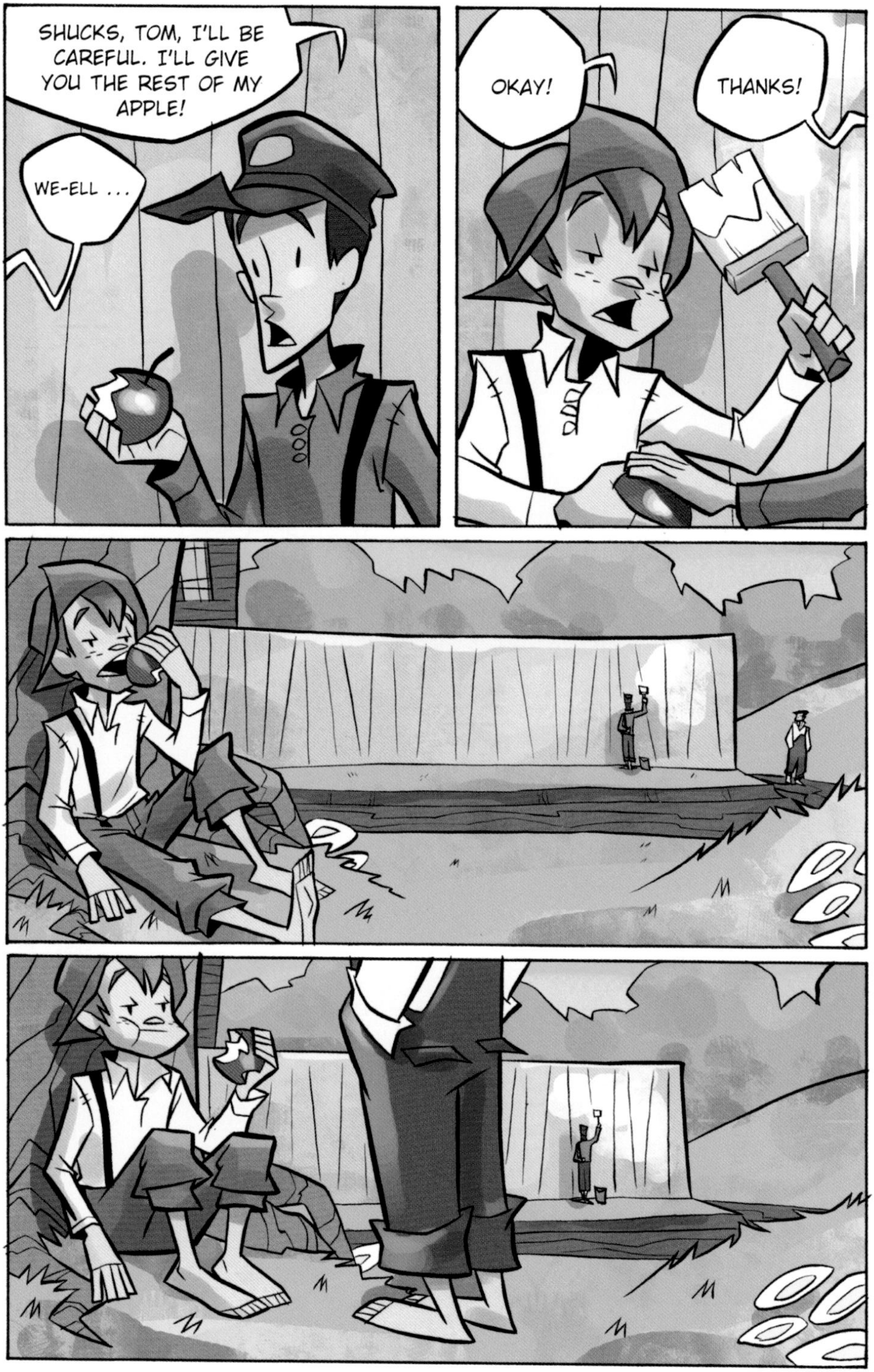
SHUCKS, TOM, I'LL BE CAREFUL. I'LL GIVE YOU THE REST OF MY APPLE!
WE-ELL . . .
OKAY!
THANKS!

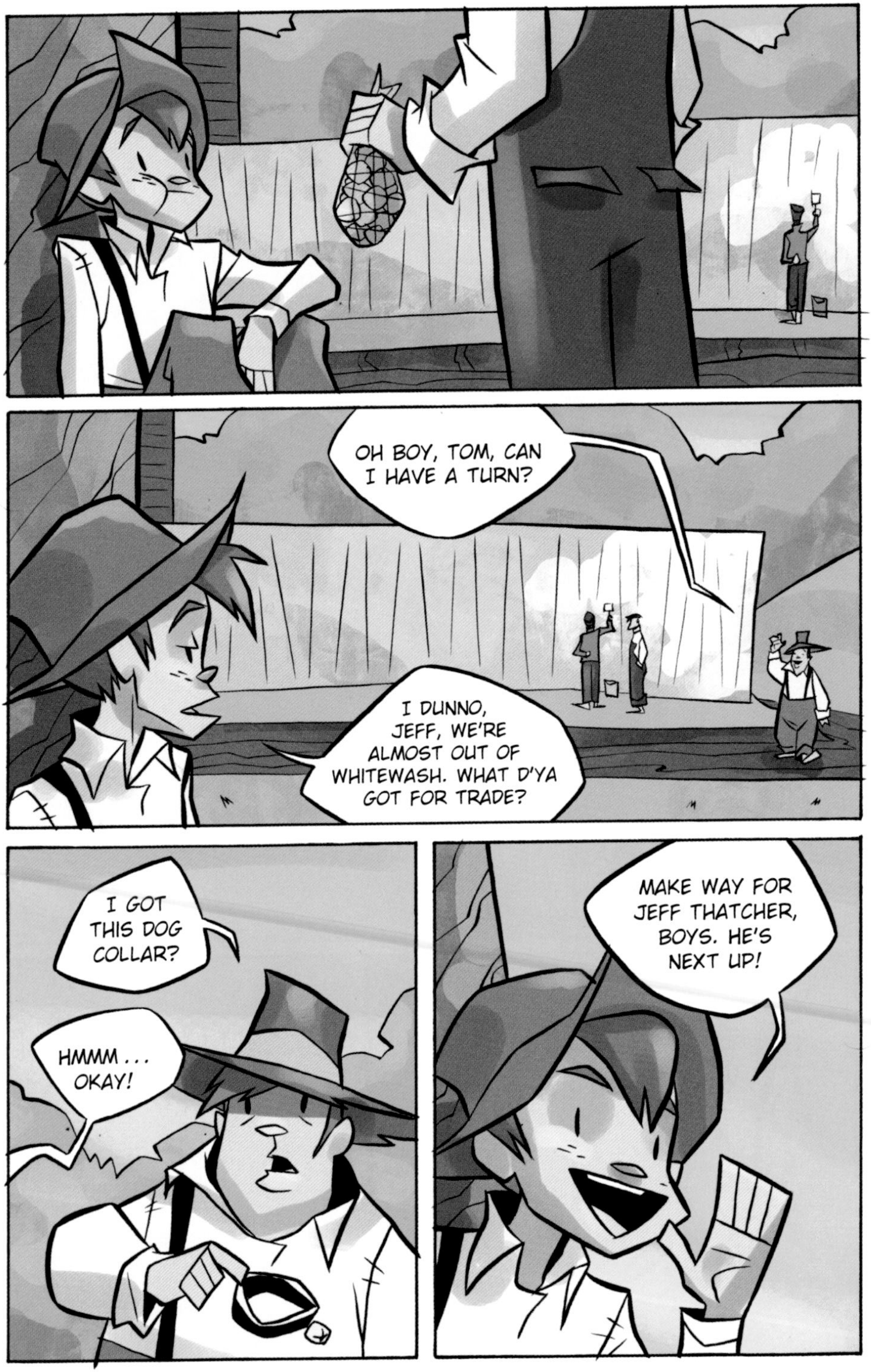
OH BOY, TOM, CAN I HAVE A TURN?
I DUNNO, JEFF, WE'RE ALMOST OUT OF WHITEWASH. WHAT D'YA GOT FOR TRADE?
I GOT THIS DOG COLLAR?
HMMM . . . OKAY!
MAKE WAY FOR JEFF THATCHER, BOYS. HE'S NEXT UP!

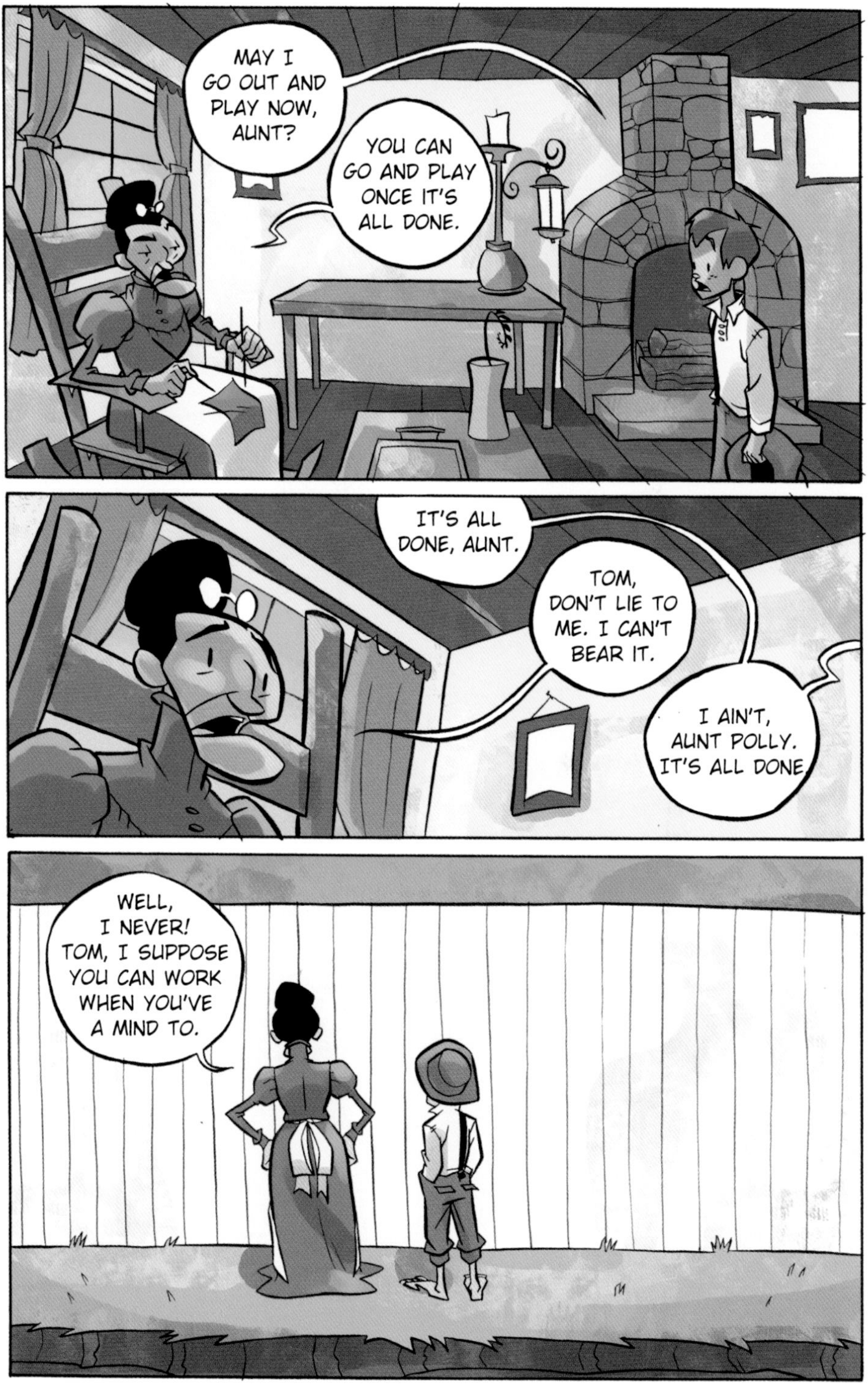
MAY I GO OUT AND PLAY NOW, AUNT?
YOU CAN GO AND PLAY ONCE IT'S ALL DONE.
IT'S ALL DONE, AUNT.
TOM, DON'T LIE TO ME. I CAN'T BEAR IT.
I AIN'T, AUNT POLLY. IT'S ALL DONE.
WELL, I NEVER! TOM, I SUPPOSE YOU CAN WORK WHEN YOU'VE A MIND TO.

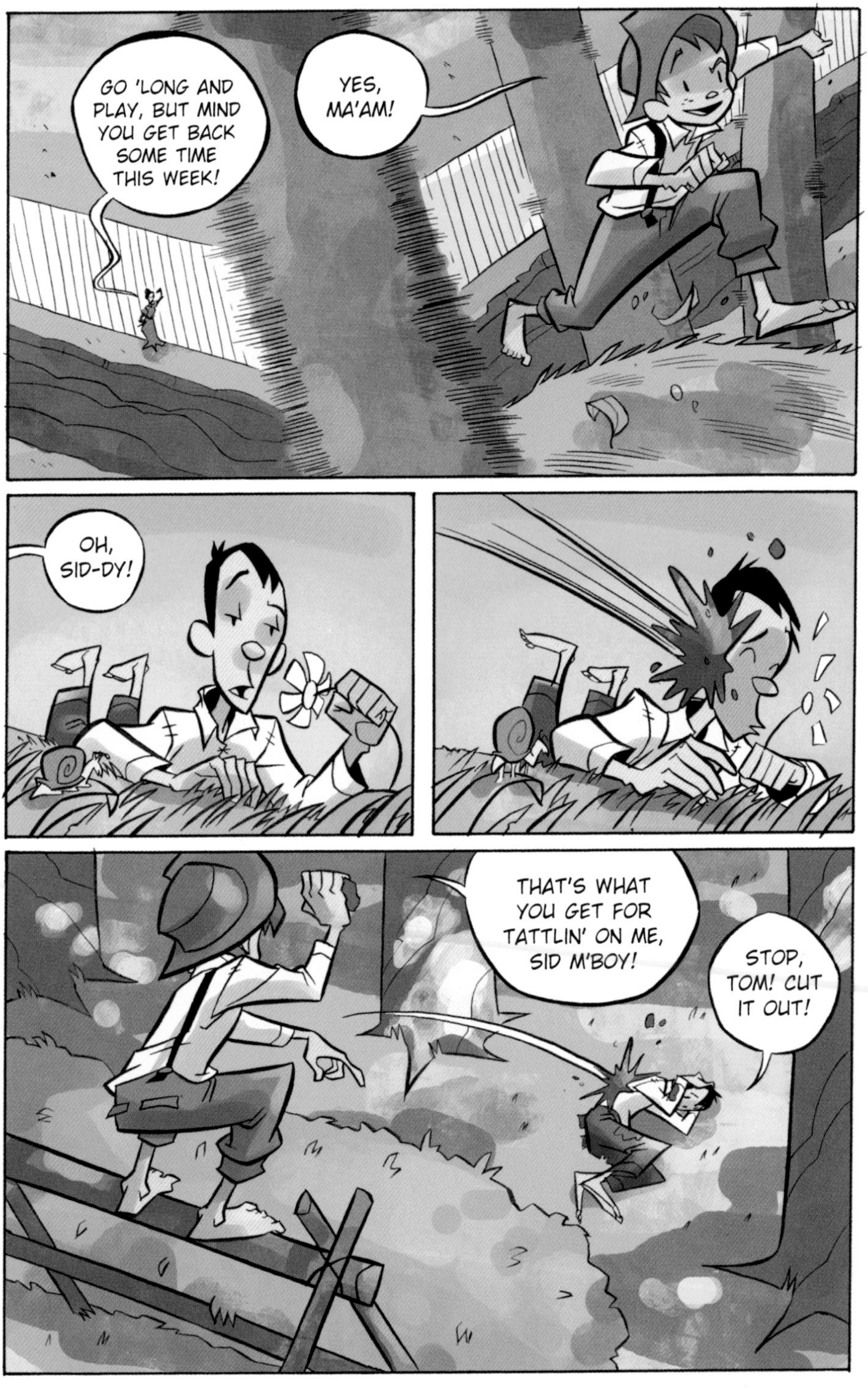
GO 'LONG AND PLAY, BUT MIND YOU GET BACK SOME TIME THIS WEEK!
YES, MA'AM!
OH, SID-DY!
THAT'S WHAT YOU GET FOR TATTLIN' ON ME, SID M'BOY!
STOP, TOM! CUT IT OUT!

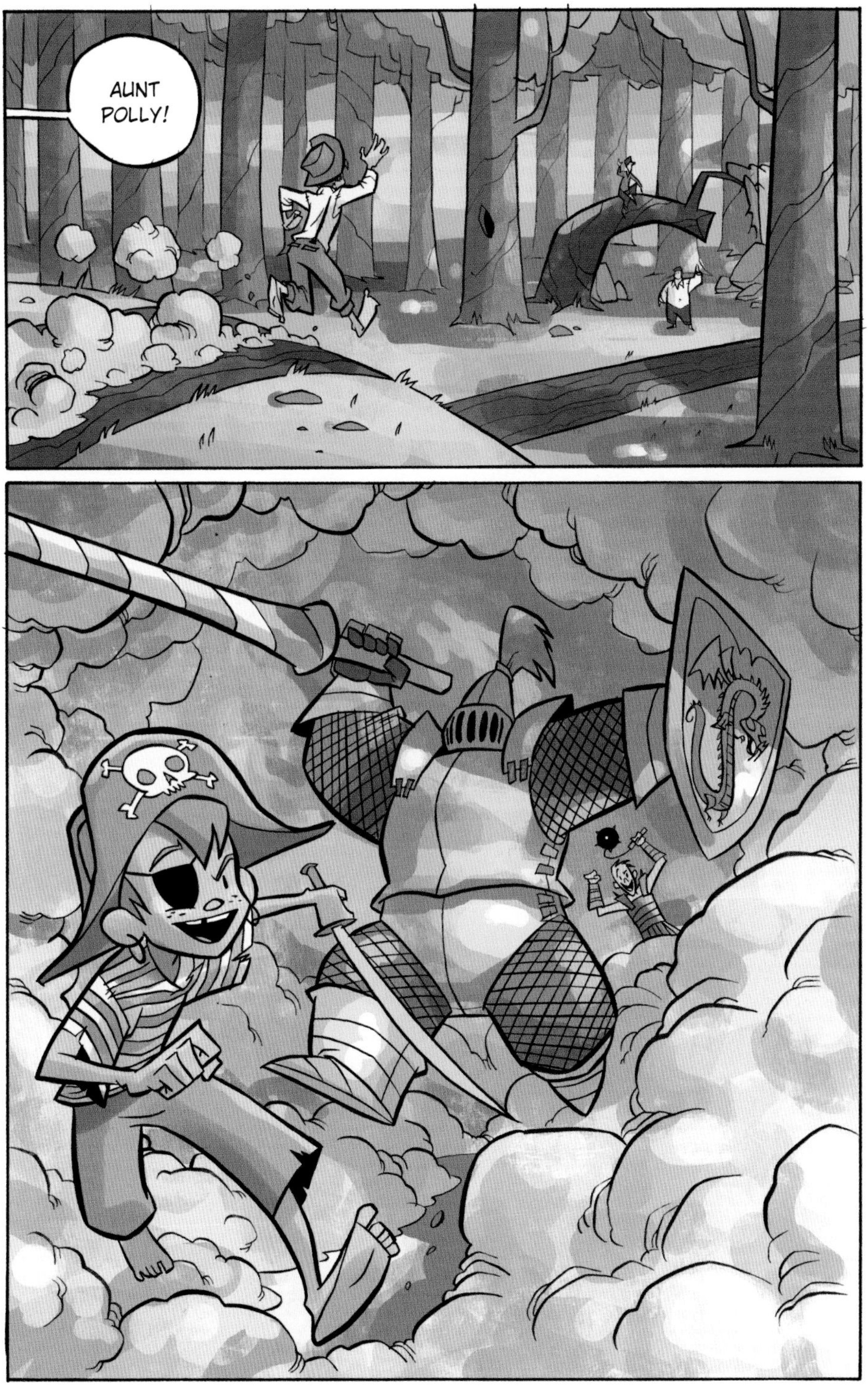
AUNT POLLY!

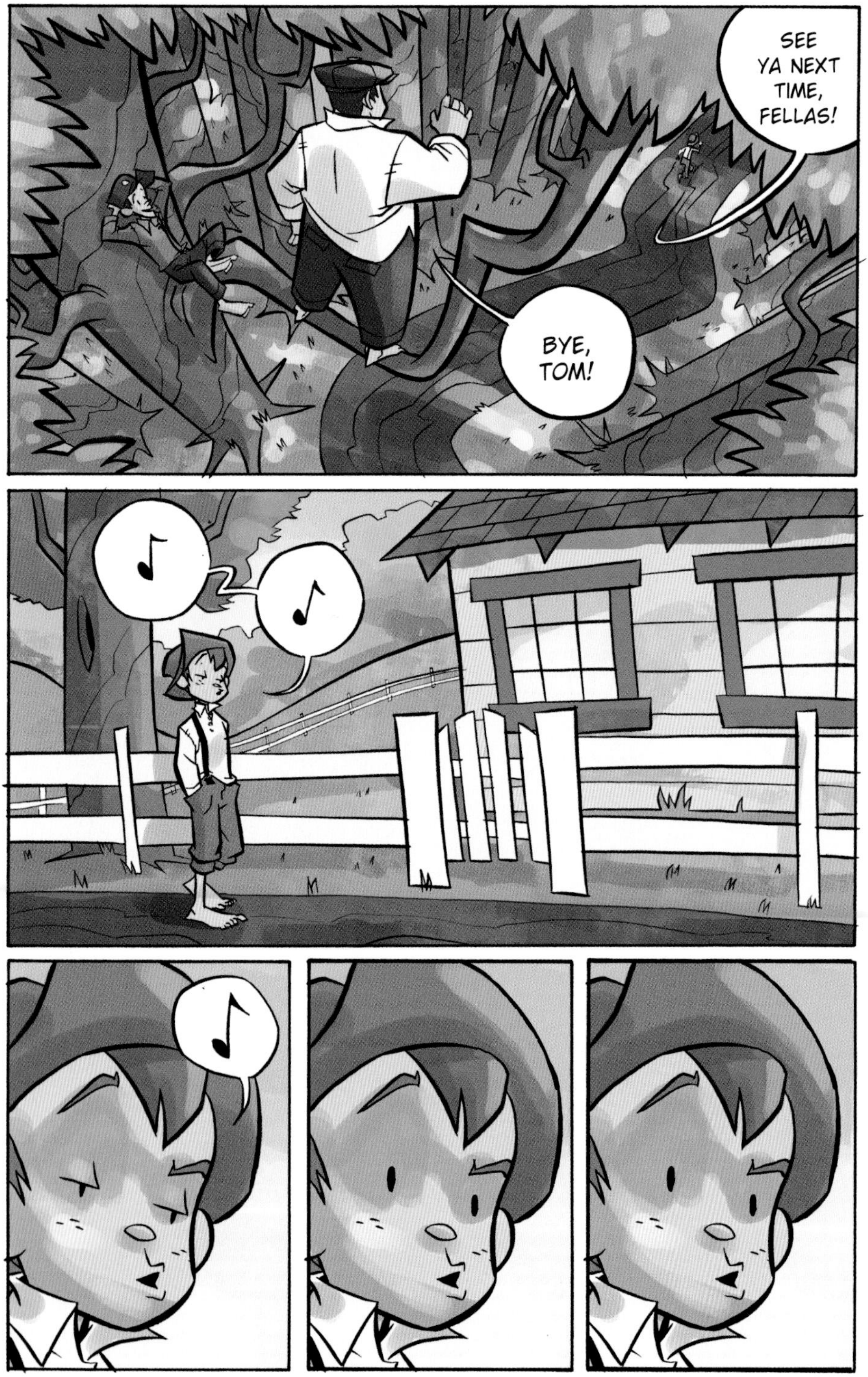
SEE YA NEXT TIME, FELLAS!
BYE, TOM!
♪
♪
♪

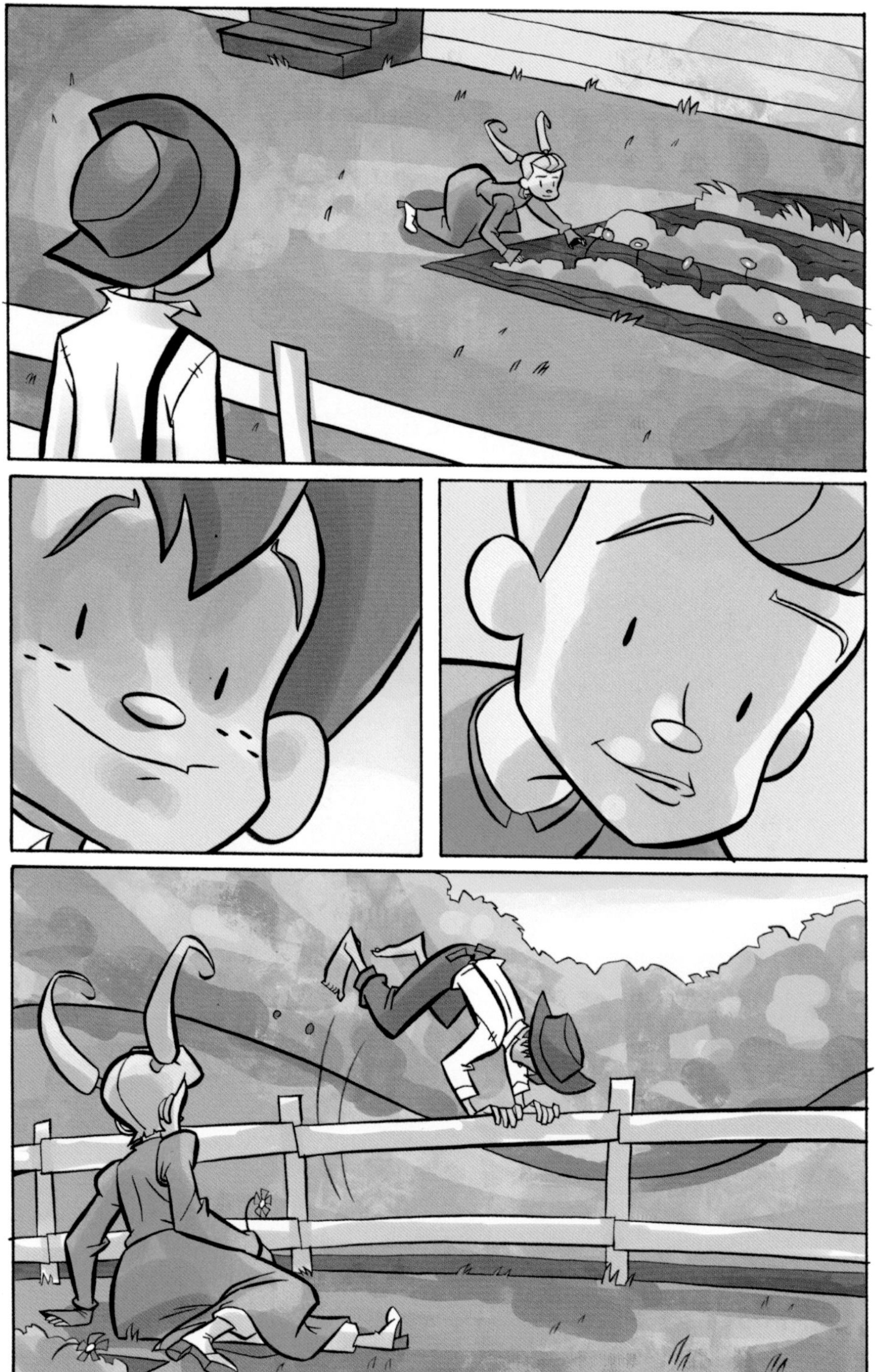

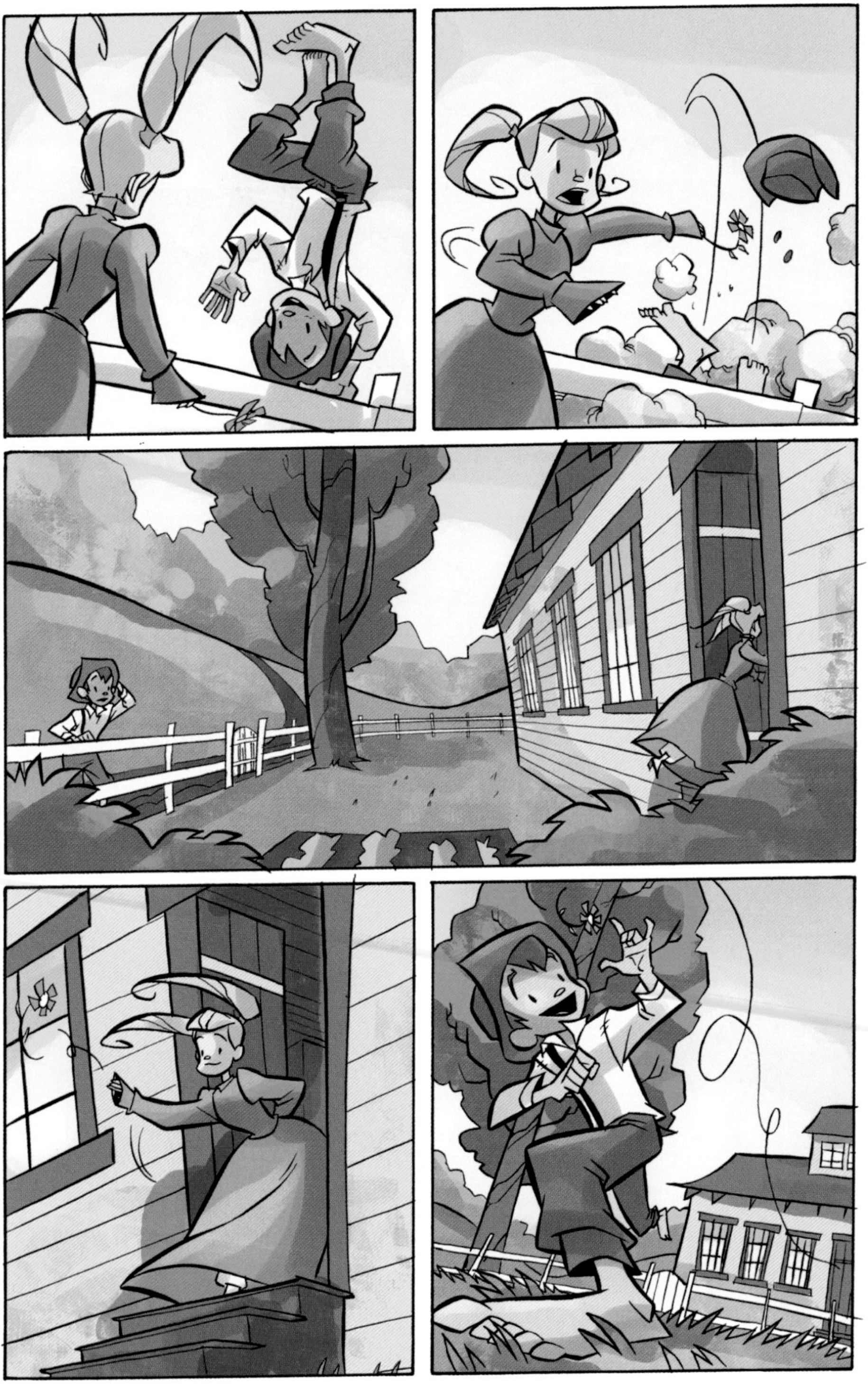

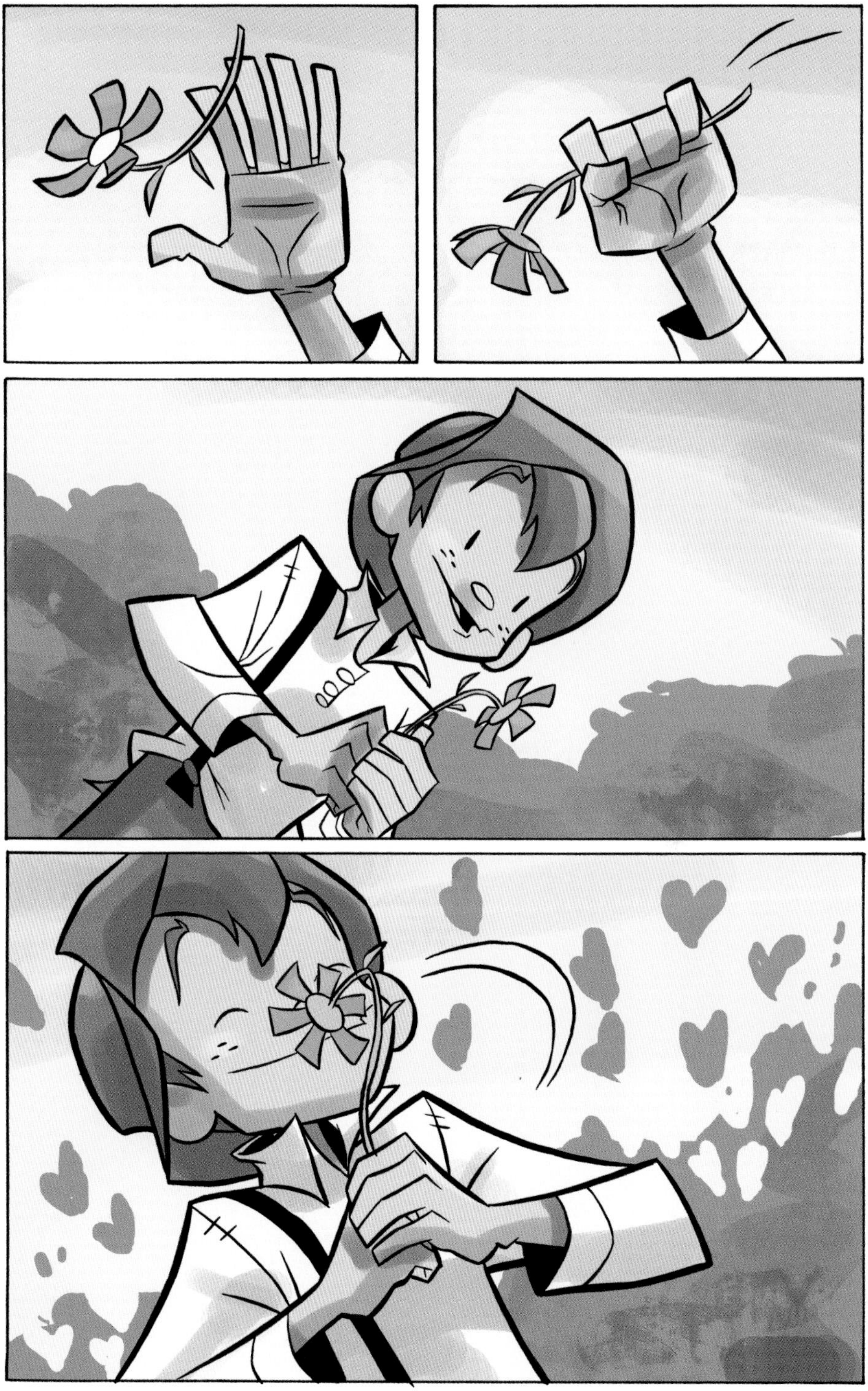

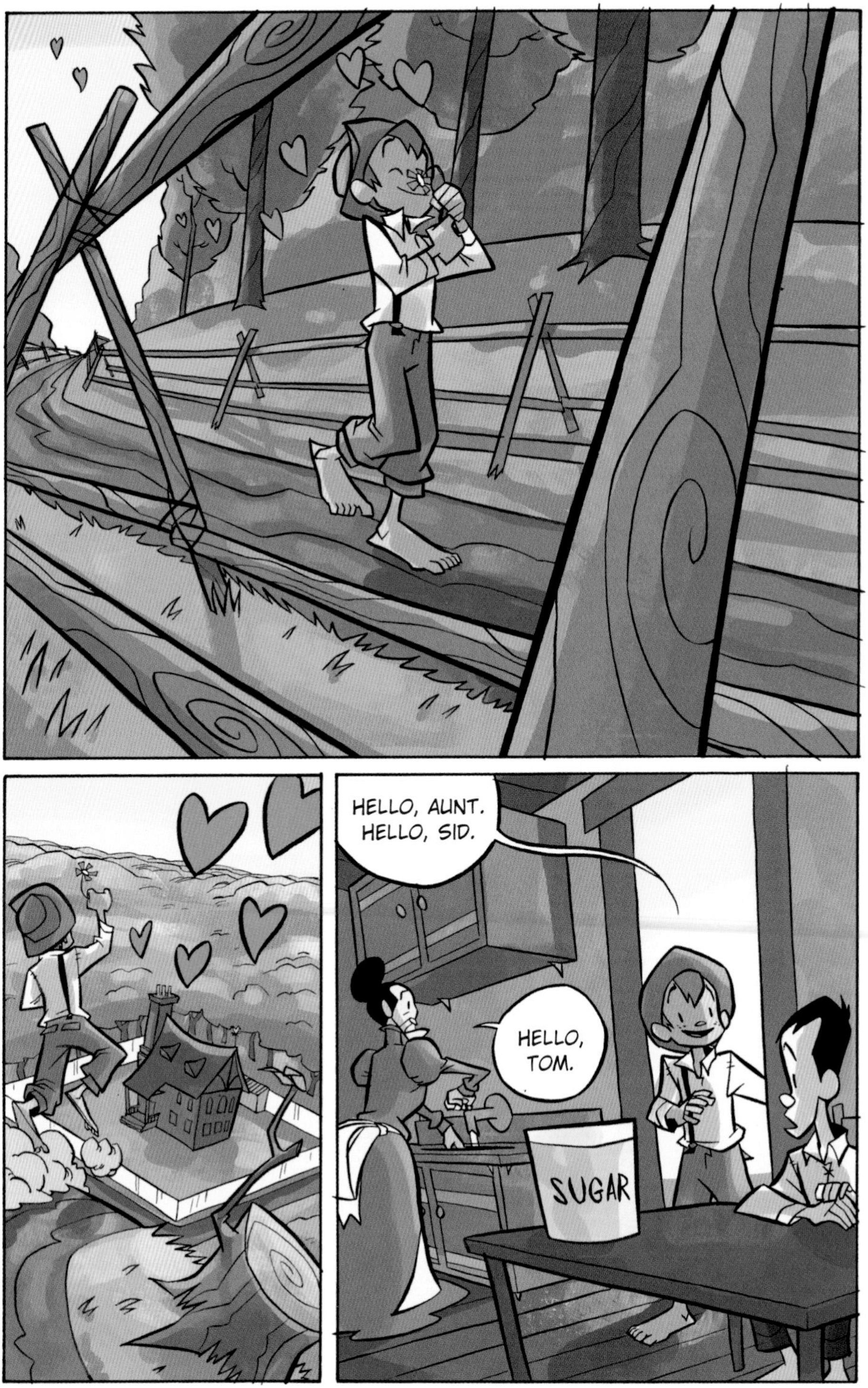
HELLO, AUNT.
HELLO, SID.
HELLO,
TOM.
SUGAR

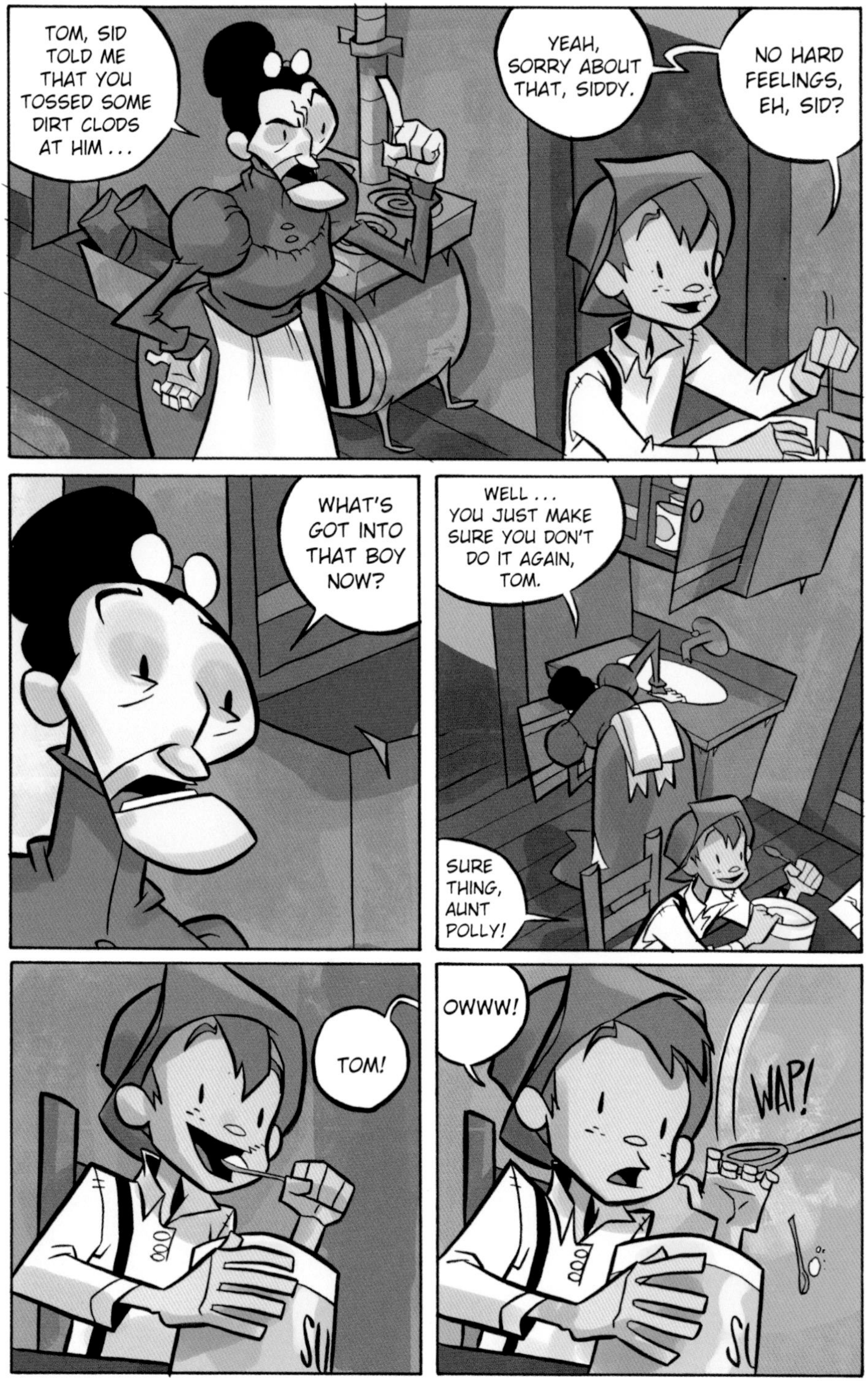
TOM, SID TOLD ME THAT YOU TOSSED SOME DIRT CLODS AT HIM . . .
YEAH, SORRY ABOUT THAT, SIDDY.
NO HARD FEELINGS, EH, SID?
WHAT'S GOT INTO THAT BOY NOW?
WELL . . . YOU JUST MAKE SURE YOU DON'T DO IT AGAIN, TOM.
SURE THING, AUNT POLLY!
TOM!
OWWW!
WAP!

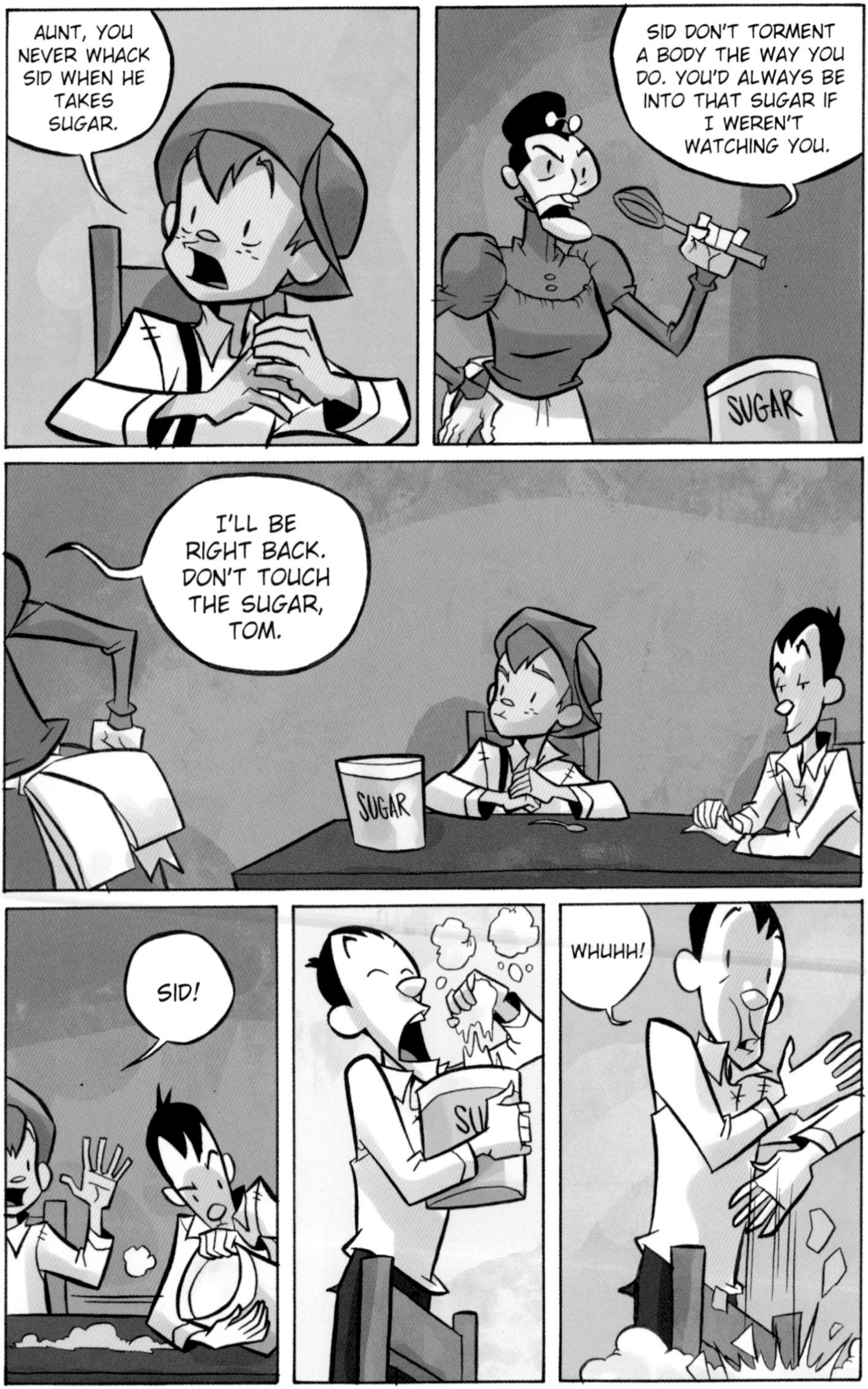
AUNT, YOU NEVER WHACK SID WHEN HE TAKES SUGAR.
SID DON'T TORMENT A BODY THE WAY YOU DO. YOU'D ALWAYS BE INTO THAT SUGAR IF I WEREN'T WATCHING YOU.
SUGAR
I'LL BE RIGHT BACK. DON'T TOUCH THE SUGAR, TOM.
SUGAR
SID!
WHUHH!

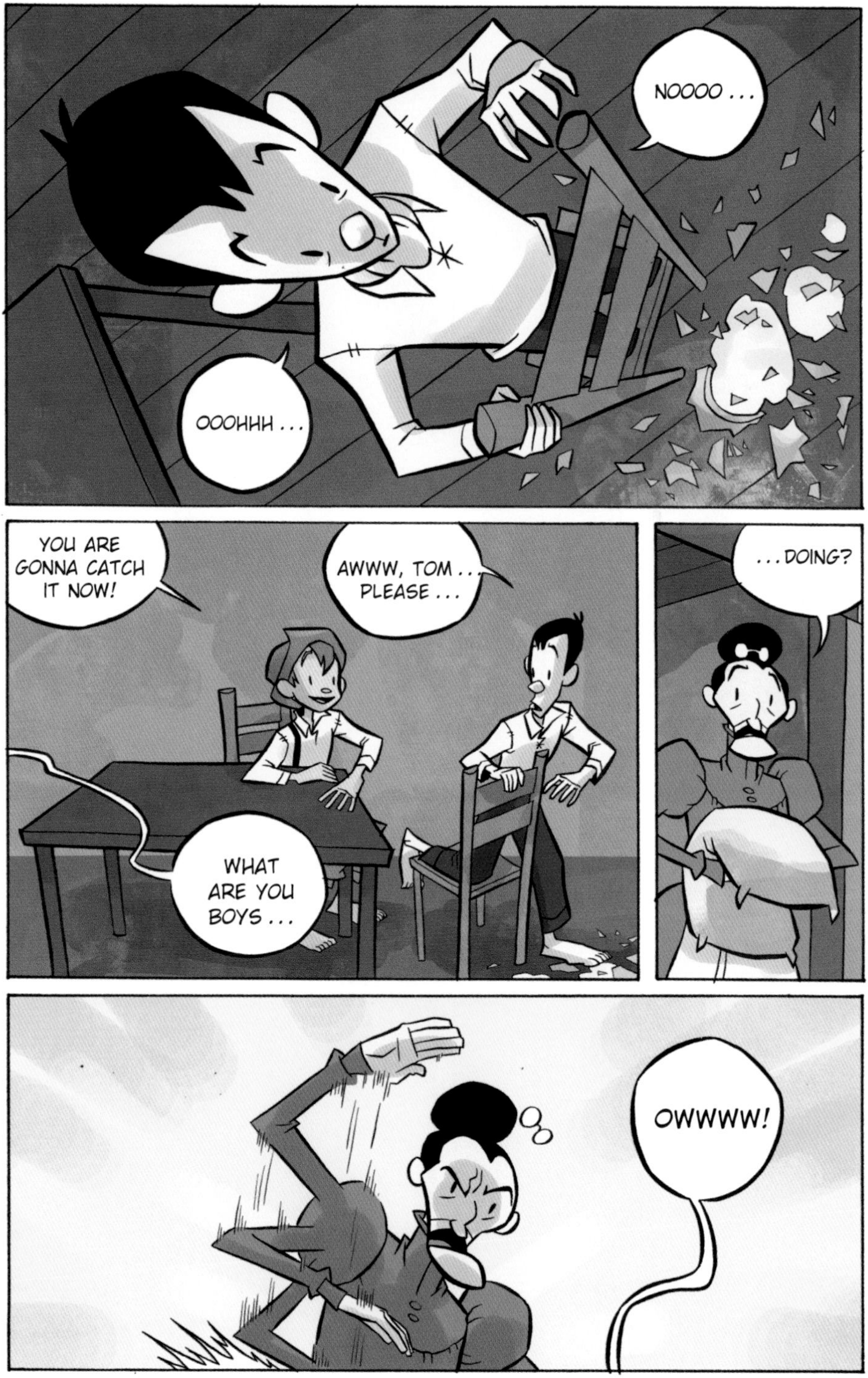
NOOOO . . .
OOOHHH . . .
YOU ARE GONNA CATCH IT NOW!
AWWW, TOM . . . PLEASE . . .
WHAT ARE YOU BOYS . . .
. . . DOING?
OWWWW!

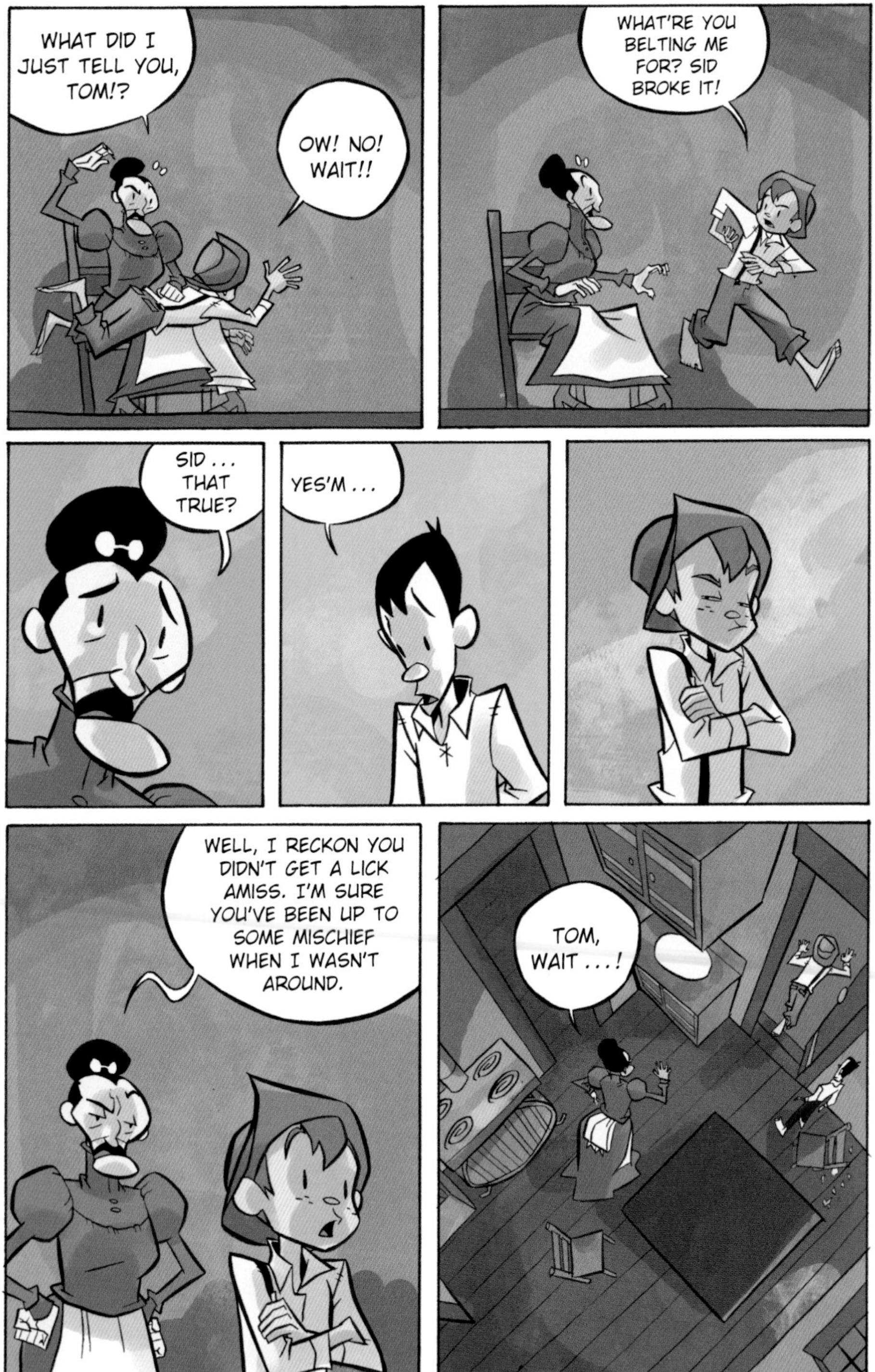
WHAT DID I JUST TELL YOU, TOM!?
OW! NO! WAIT!!
WHAT'RE YOU BELTING ME FOR? SID BROKE IT!
SID . . . THAT TRUE?
YES'M . . .
WELL, I RECKON YOU DIDN'T GET A LICK AMISS. I'M SURE YOU'VE BEEN UP TO SOME MISCHIEF WHEN I WASN'T AROUND.
TOM, WAIT . . . !

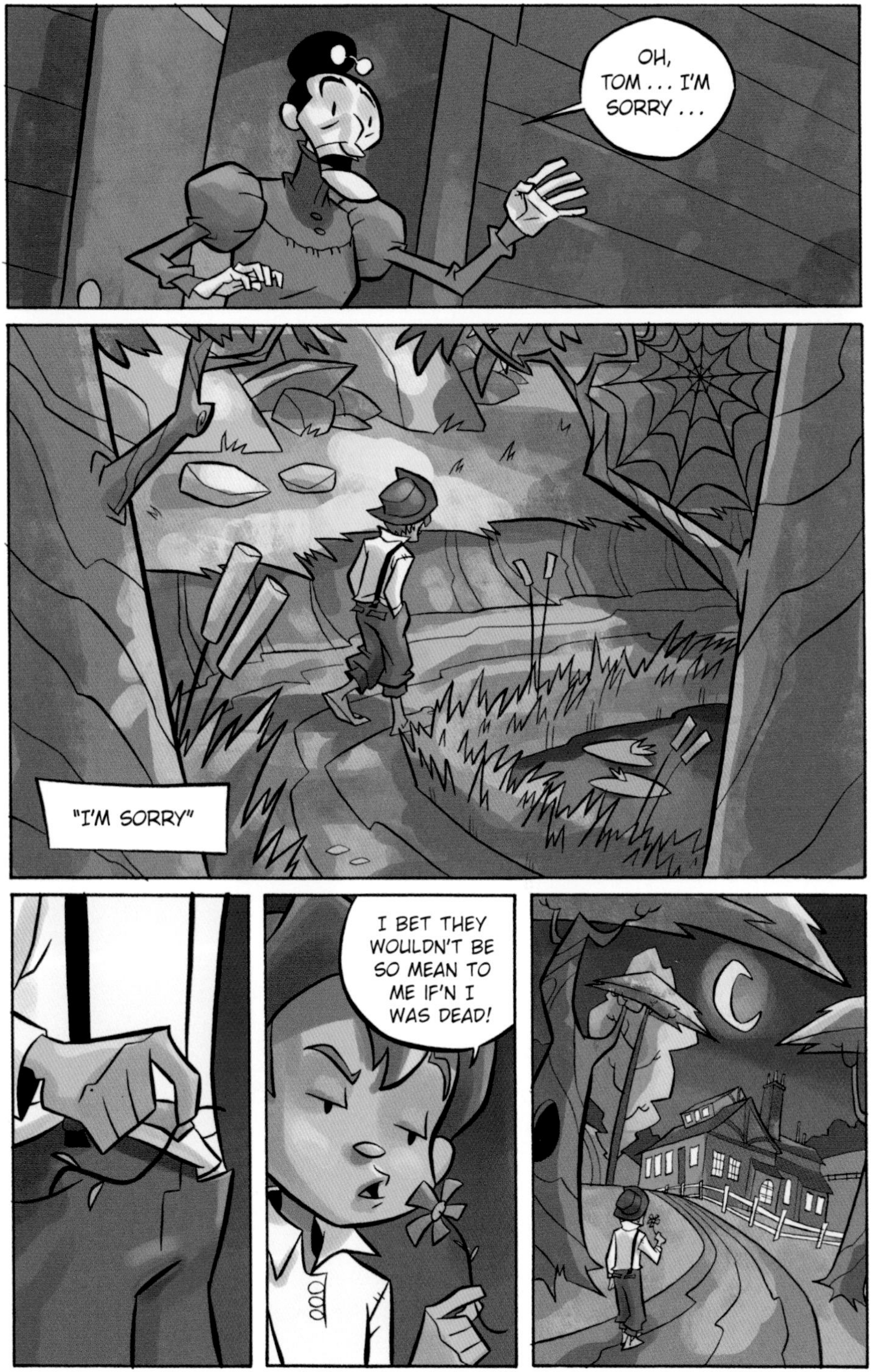

OH, TOM . . . I'M SORRY . . .
"I'M SORRY"
I BET THEY WOULDN'T BE SO MEAN TO ME IF'N I WAS DEAD!

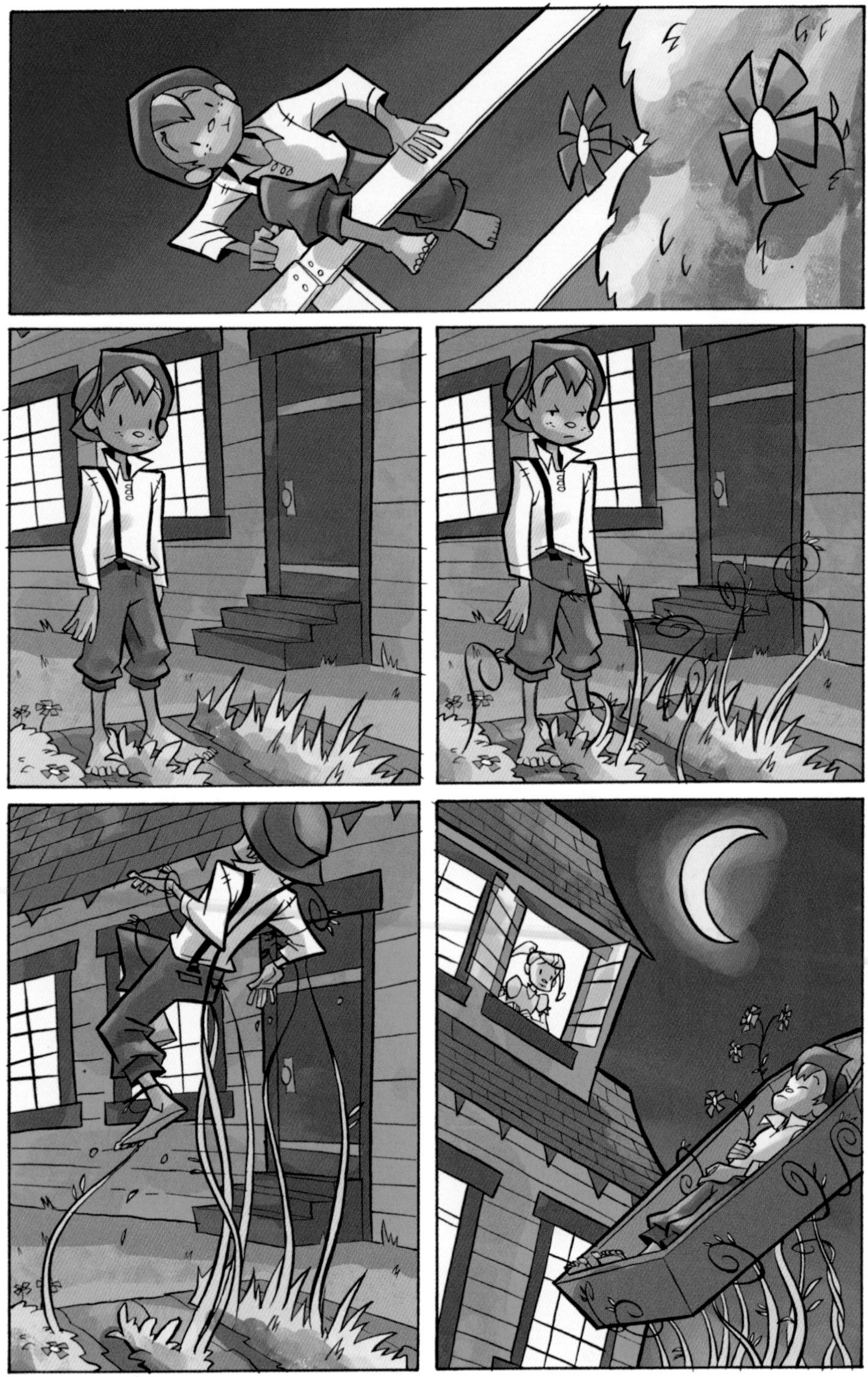

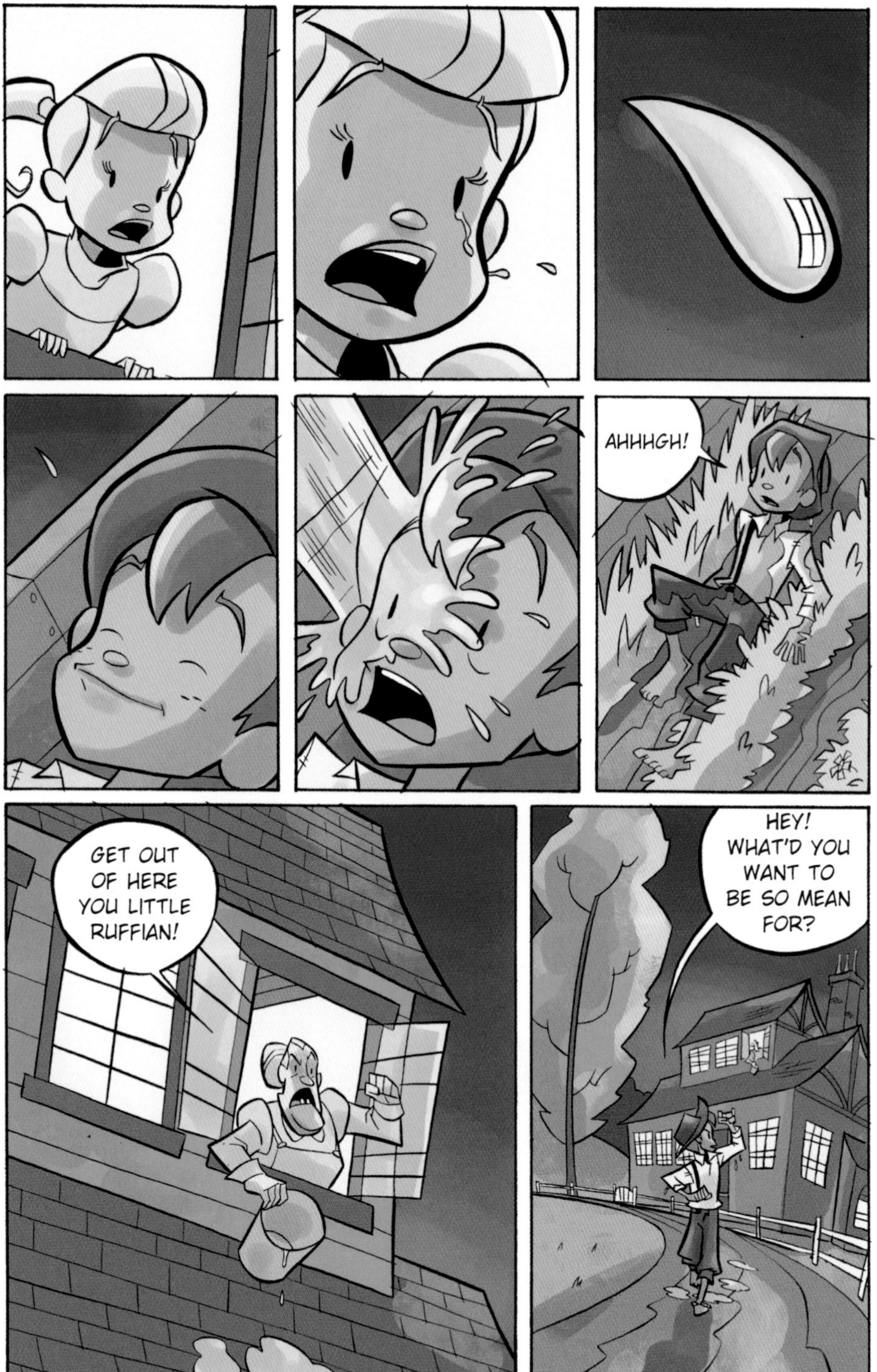
AHHHGH!
GET OUT OF HERE YOU LITTLE RUFFIAN!
HEY! WHAT'D YOU WANT TO BE SO MEAN FOR?

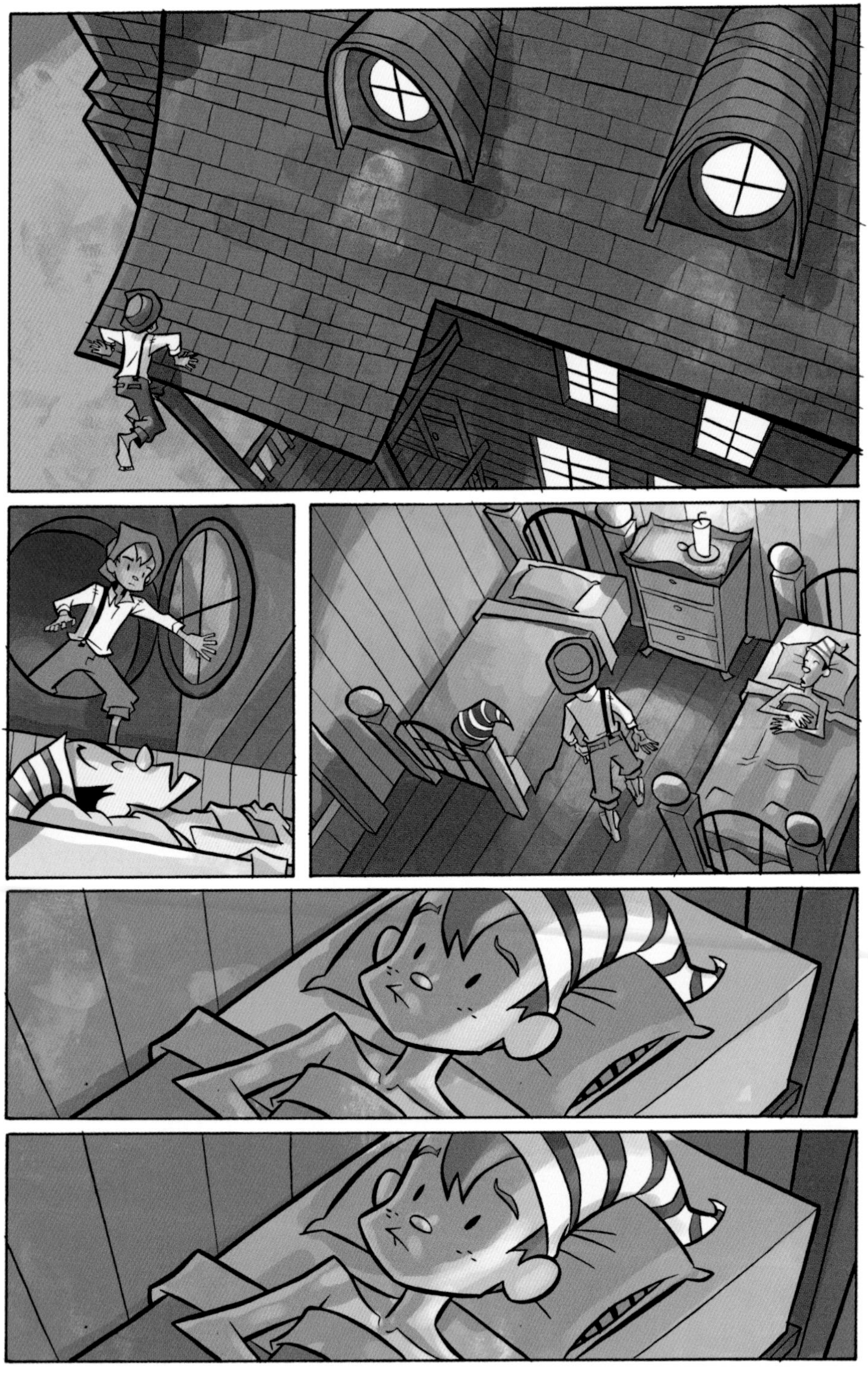

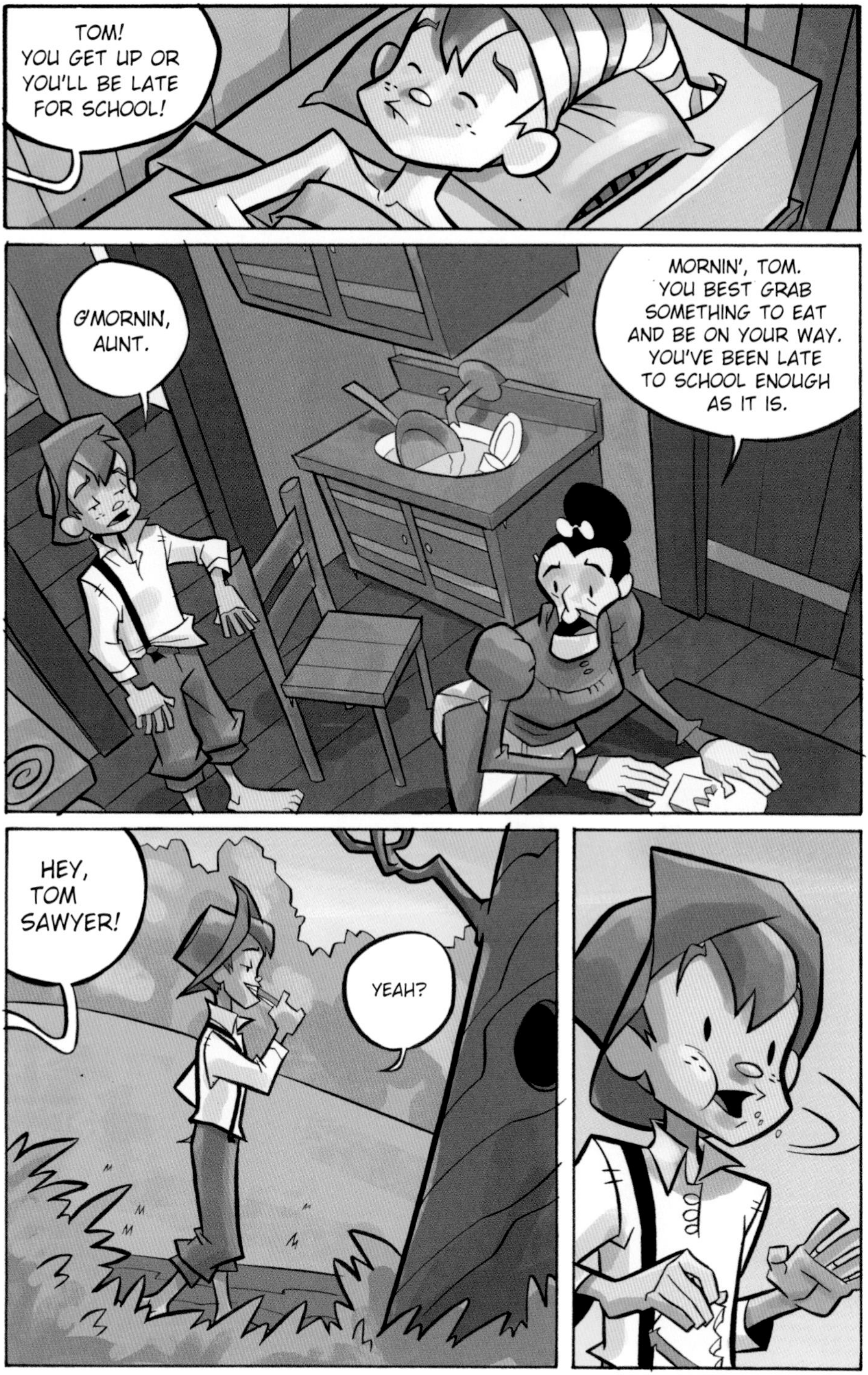
TOM! YOU GET UP OR YOU'LL BE LATE FOR SCHOOL!
G'MORNIN, AUNT.
MORNIN', TOM. YOU BEST GRAB SOMETHING TO EAT AND BE ON YOUR WAY. YOU'VE BEEN LATE TO SCHOOL ENOUGH AS IT IS.
HEY, TOM SAWYER!
YEAH?

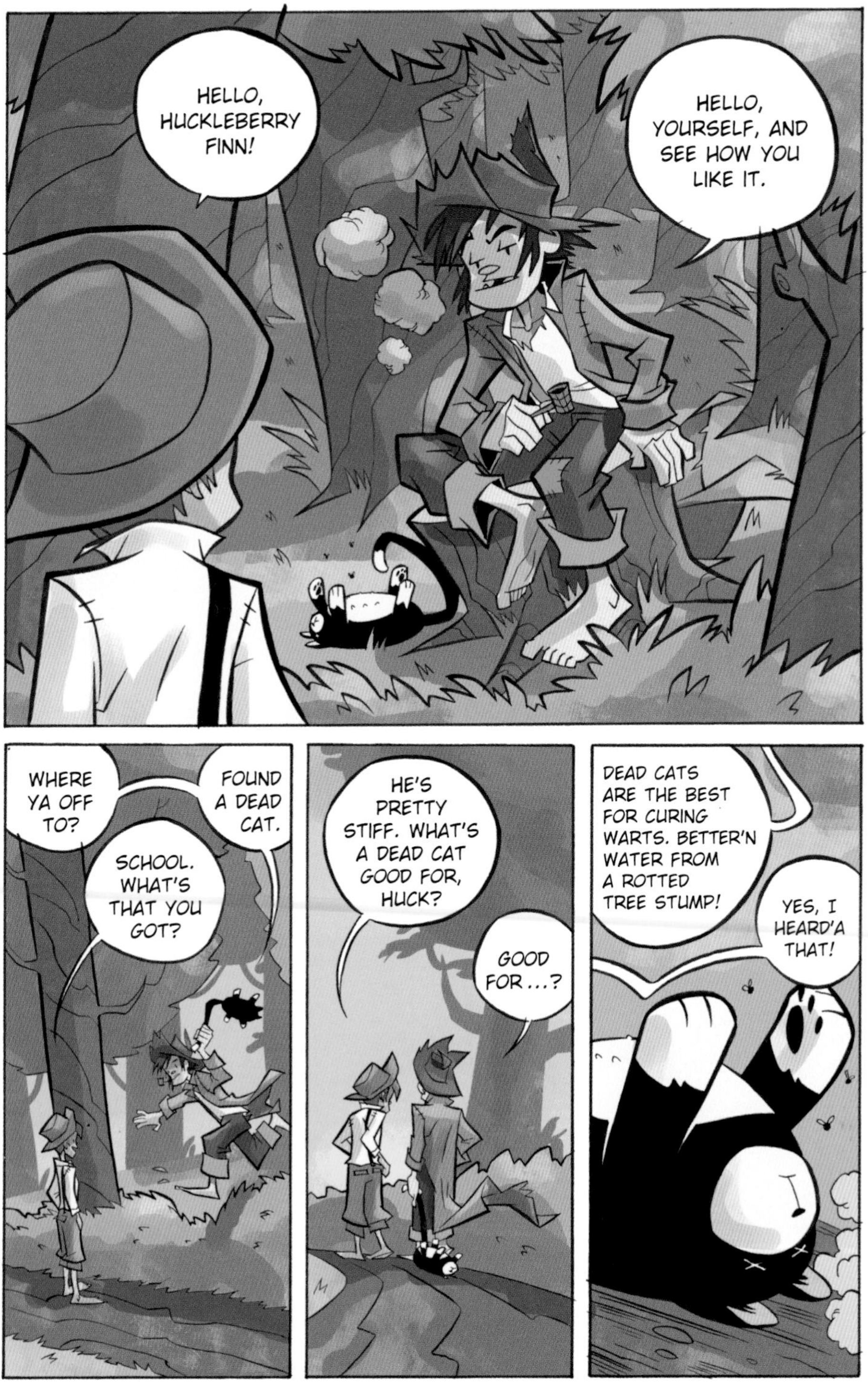
HELLO, HUCKLEBERRY FINN!
HELLO, YOURSELF, AND SEE HOW YOU LIKE IT.
WHERE YA OFF TO?
SCHOOL. WHAT'S THAT YOU GOT?
FOUND A DEAD CAT.
HE'S PRETTY STIFF. WHAT'S A DEAD CAT GOOD FOR, HUCK?
GOOD FOR...?
DEAD CATS ARE THE BEST FOR CURING WARTS. BETTER'N WATER FROM A ROTTED TREE STUMP!
YES, I HEARD'A THAT!

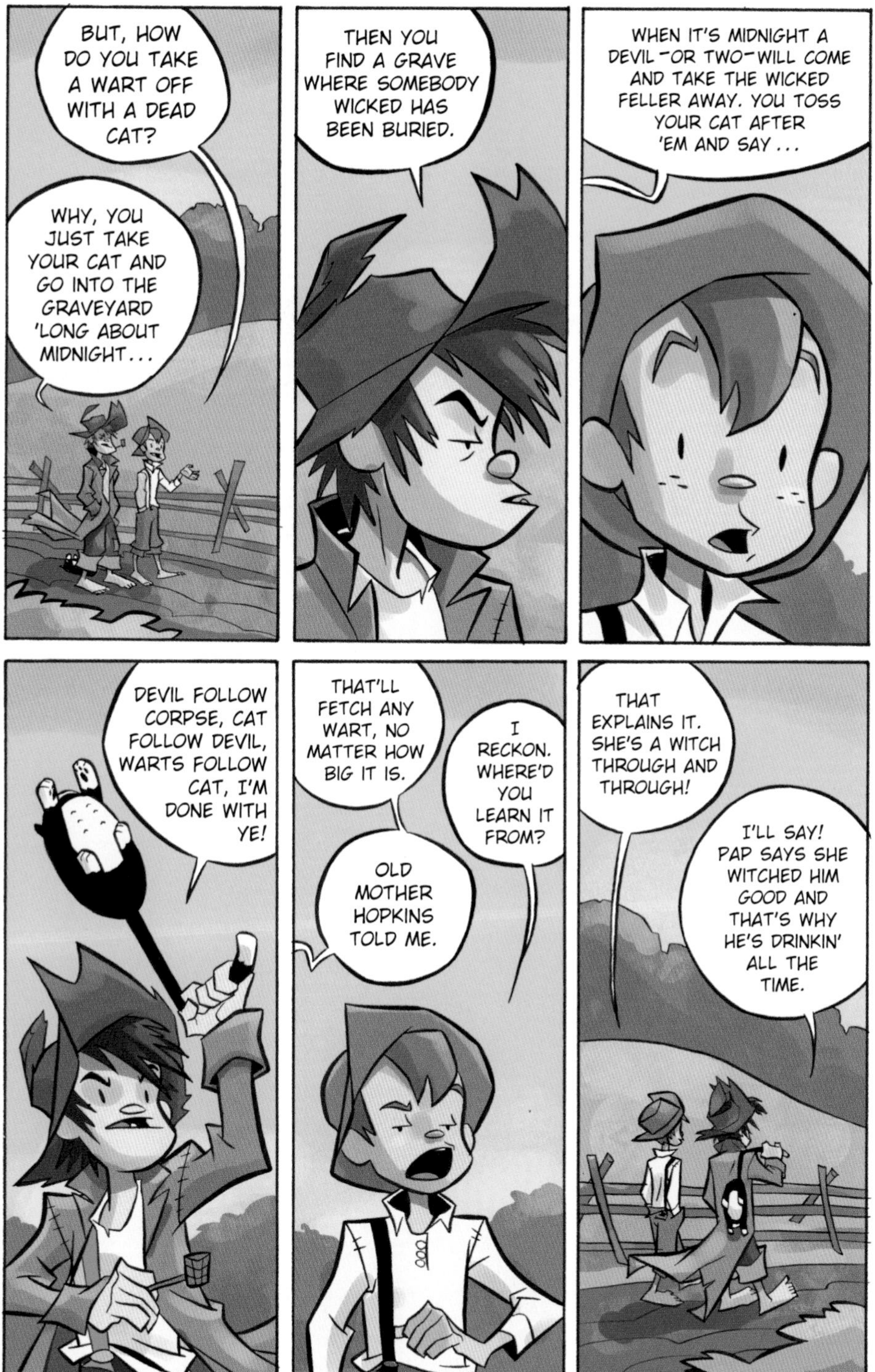
BUT, HOW DO YOU TAKE A WART OFF WITH A DEAD CAT?
WHY, YOU JUST TAKE YOUR CAT AND GO INTO THE GRAVEYARD 'LONG ABOUT MIDNIGHT...
THEN YOU FIND A GRAVE WHERE SOMEBODY WICKED HAS BEEN BURIED.
WHEN IT'S MIDNIGHT A DEVIL—OR TWO—WILL COME AND TAKE THE WICKED FELLER AWAY. YOU TOSS YOUR CAT AFTER 'EM AND SAY...
DEVIL FOLLOW CORPSE, CAT FOLLOW DEVIL, WARTS FOLLOW CAT, I'M DONE WITH YE!
THAT'LL FETCH ANY WART, NO MATTER HOW BIG IT IS.
I RECKON. WHERE'D YOU LEARN IT FROM?
OLD MOTHER HOPKINS TOLD ME.
THAT EXPLAINS IT. SHE'S A WITCH THROUGH AND THROUGH!
I'LL SAY! PAP SAYS SHE WITCHED HIM GOOD AND THAT'S WHY HE'S DRINKIN' ALL THE TIME.

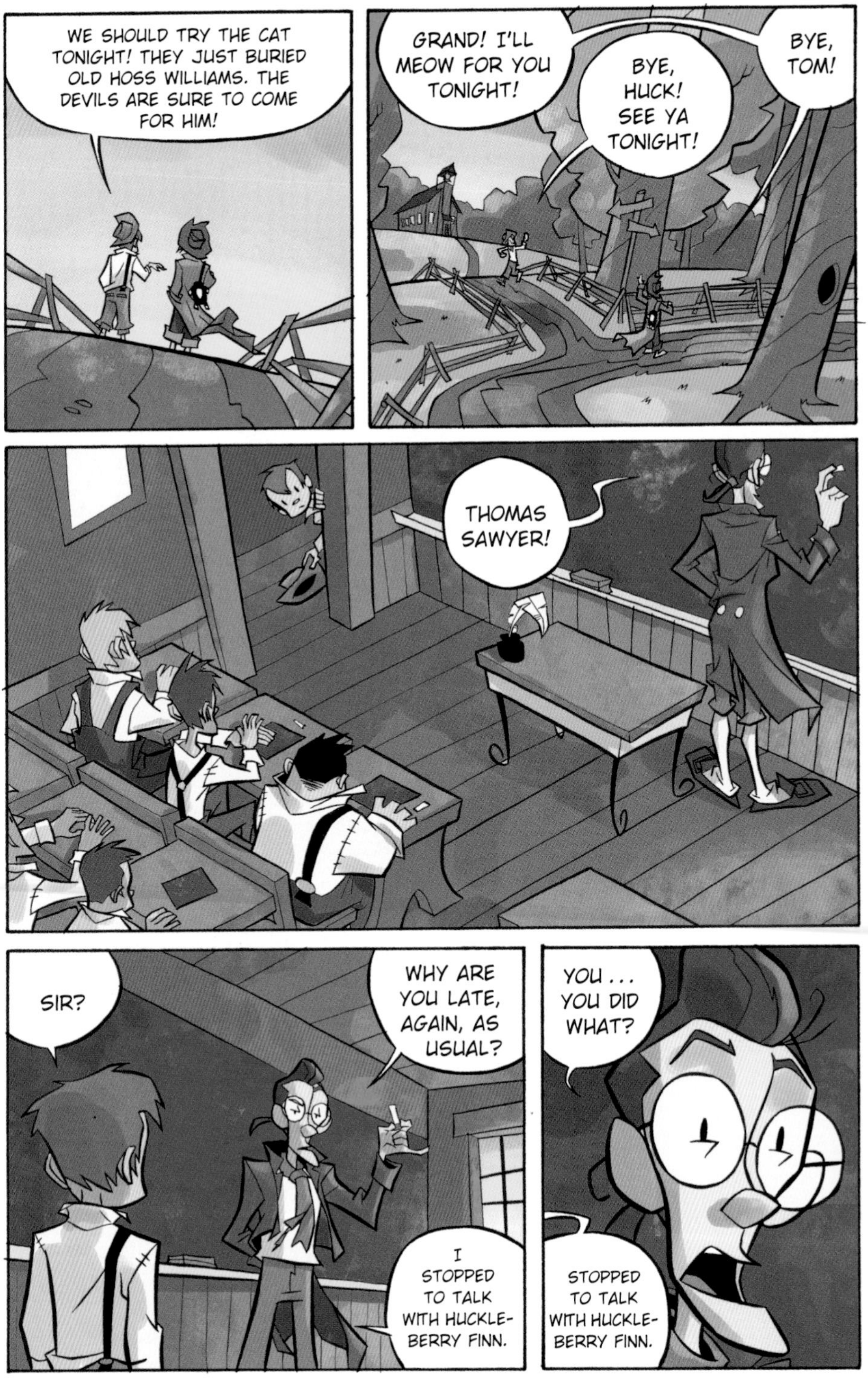
WE SHOULD TRY THE CAT TONIGHT! THEY JUST BURIED OLD HOSS WILLIAMS. THE DEVILS ARE SURE TO COME FOR HIM!
GRAND! I'LL MEOW FOR YOU TONIGHT!
BYE, HUCK! SEE YA TONIGHT!
BYE, TOM!
THOMAS SAWYER!
SIR?
WHY ARE YOU LATE, AGAIN, AS USUAL?
I STOPPED TO TALK WITH HUCKLE-BERRY FINN.
YOU . . . YOU DID WHAT?
STOPPED TO TALK WITH HUCKLE-BERRY FINN.

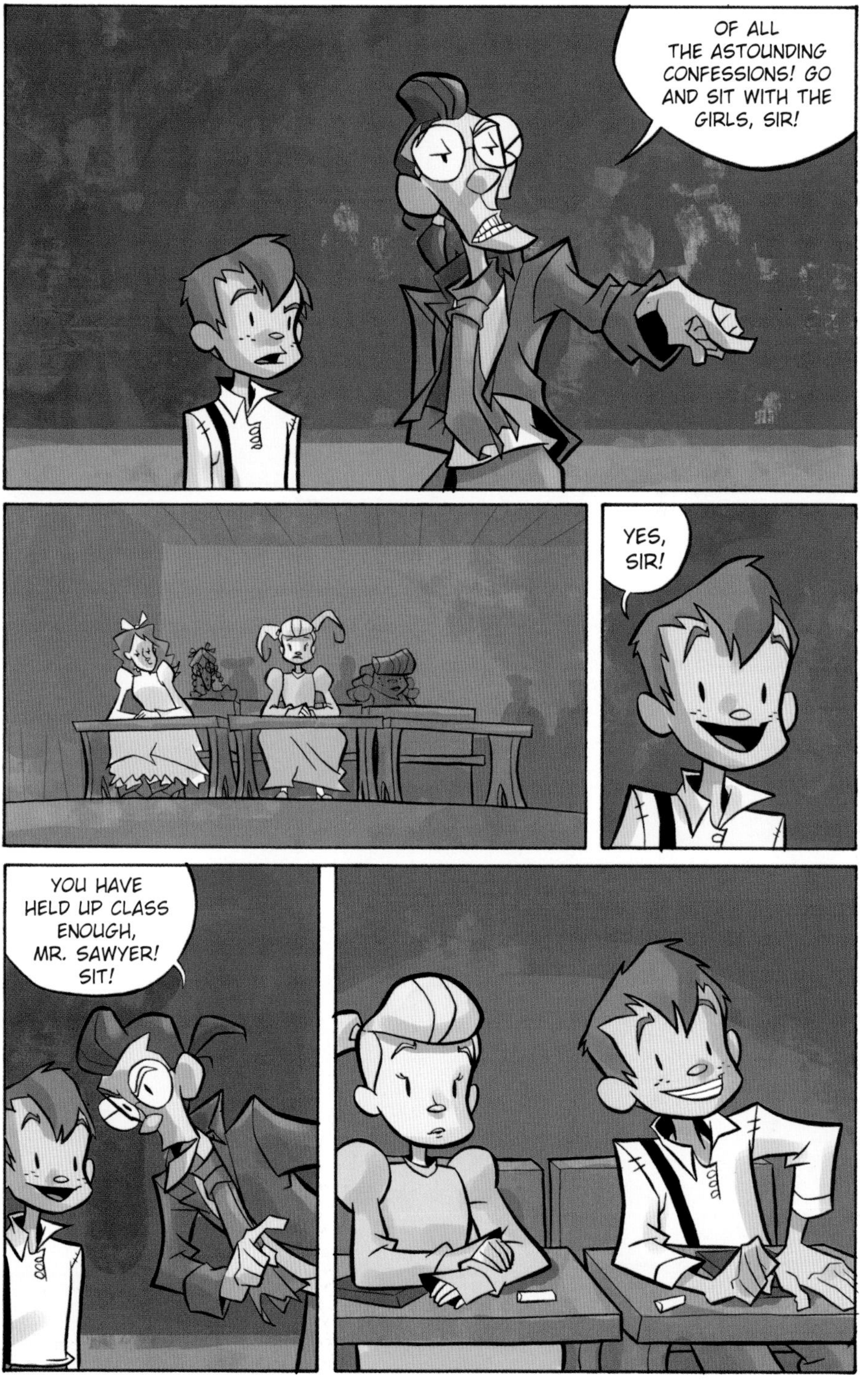
OF ALL THE ASTOUNDING CONFESSIONS! GO AND SIT WITH THE GIRLS, SIR!
YES, SIR!
YOU HAVE HELD UP CLASS ENOUGH, MR. SAWYER! SIT!

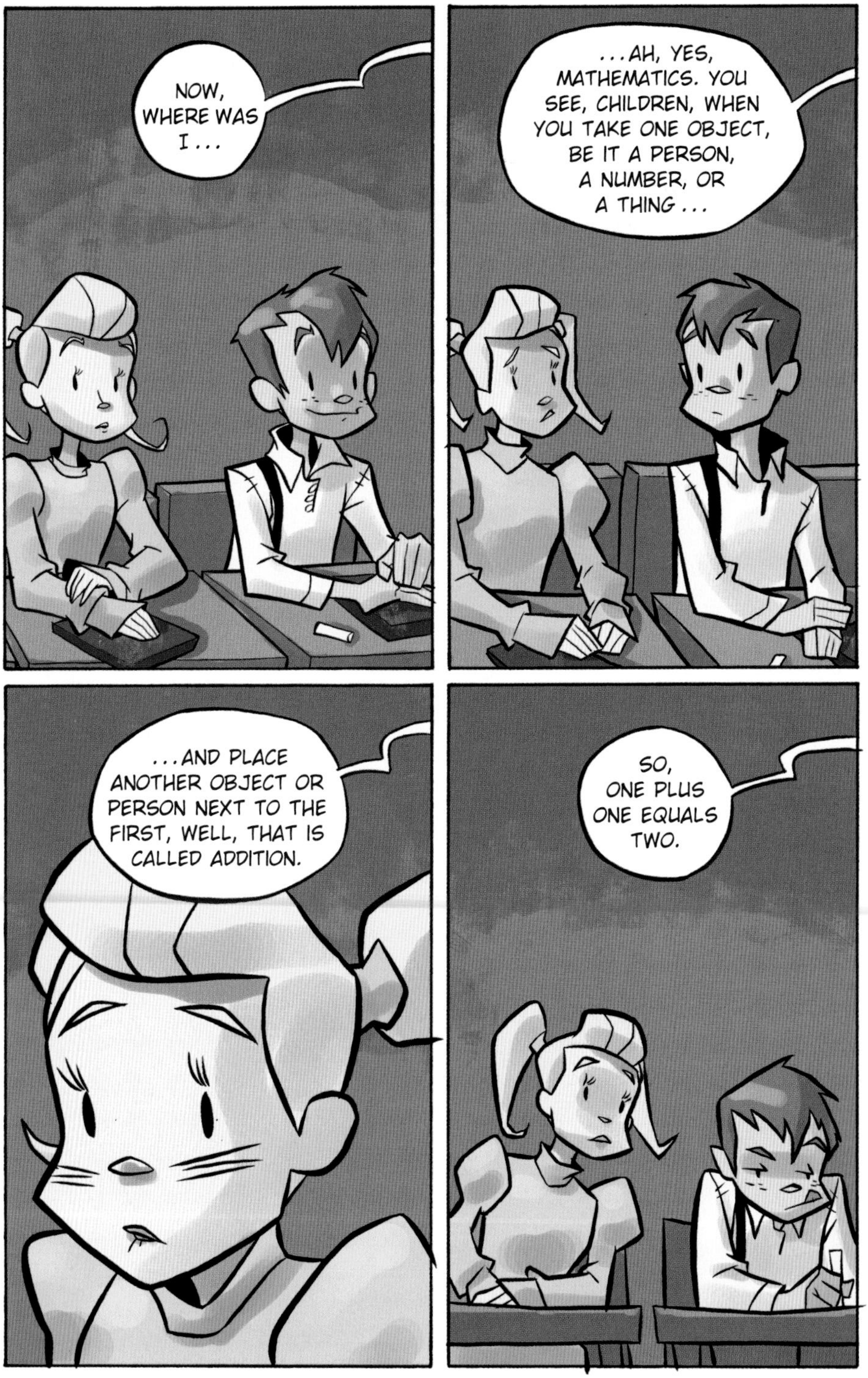
NOW, WHERE WAS I . . .
. . . AH, YES, MATHEMATICS. YOU SEE, CHILDREN, WHEN YOU TAKE ONE OBJECT, BE IT A PERSON, A NUMBER, OR A THING . . .
. . . AND PLACE ANOTHER OBJECT OR PERSON NEXT TO THE FIRST, WELL, THAT IS CALLED ADDITION.
SO, ONE PLUS ONE EQUALS TWO.

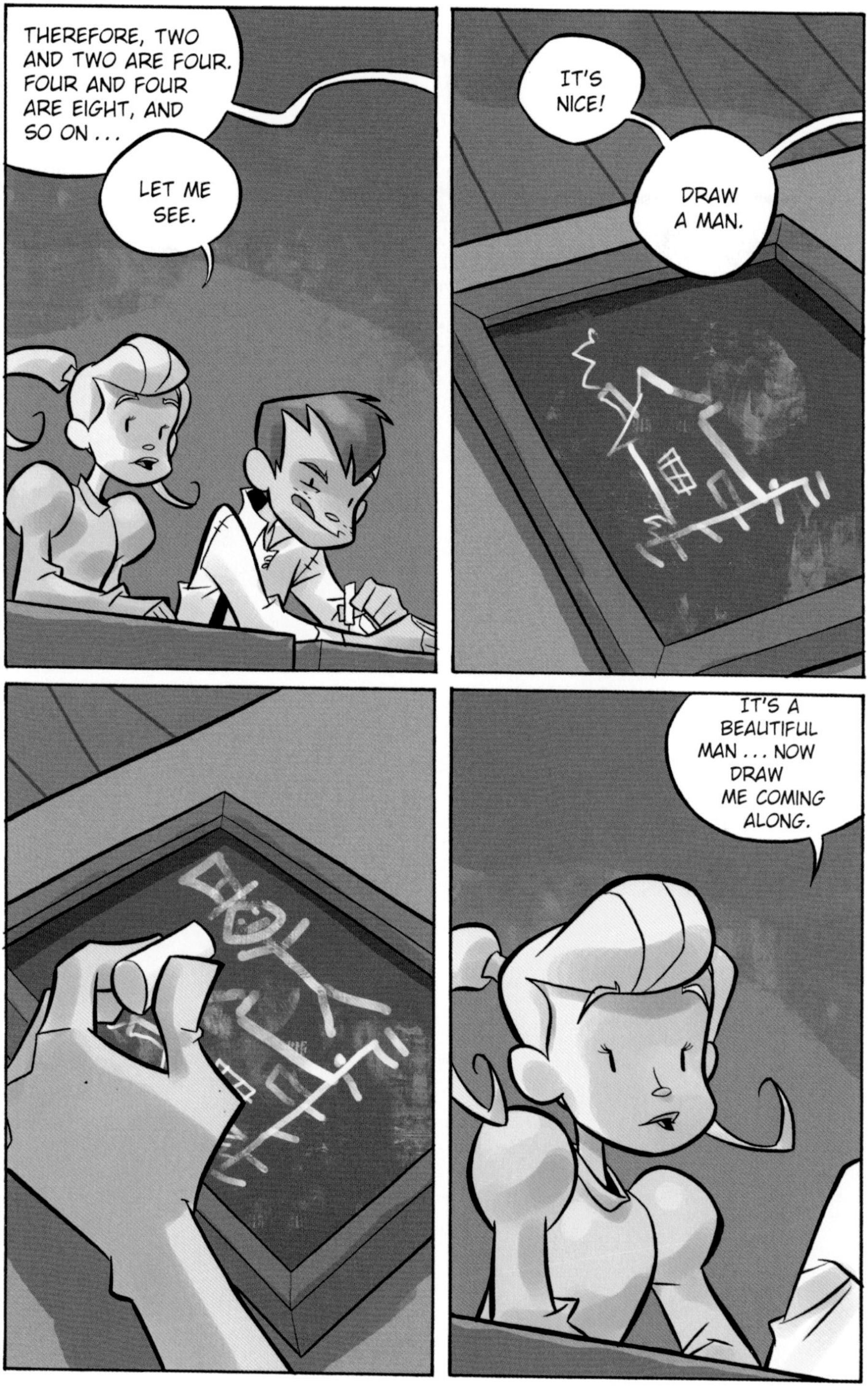
THEREFORE, TWO AND TWO ARE FOUR. FOUR AND FOUR ARE EIGHT, AND SO ON . . .
LET ME SEE.
IT'S NICE!
DRAW A MAN.
IT'S A BEAUTIFUL MAN . . . NOW DRAW ME COMING ALONG.

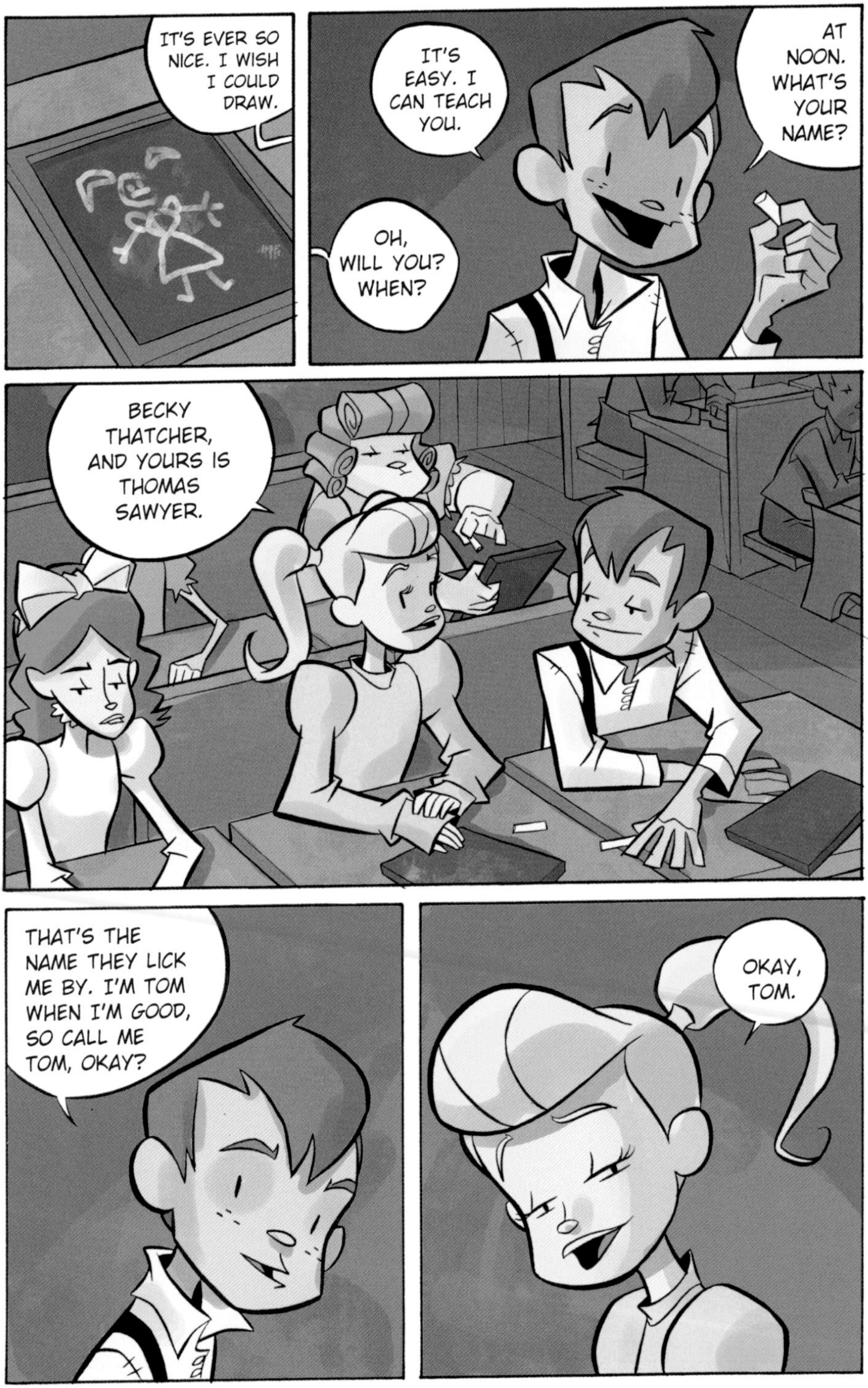
IT'S EVER SO NICE. I WISH I COULD DRAW.
IT'S EASY. I CAN TEACH YOU.
OH, WILL YOU? WHEN?
AT NOON. WHAT'S YOUR NAME?
BECKY THATCHER, AND YOURS IS THOMAS SAWYER.
THAT'S THE NAME THEY LICK ME BY. I'M TOM WHEN I'M GOOD, SO CALL ME TOM, OKAY?
OKAY, TOM.

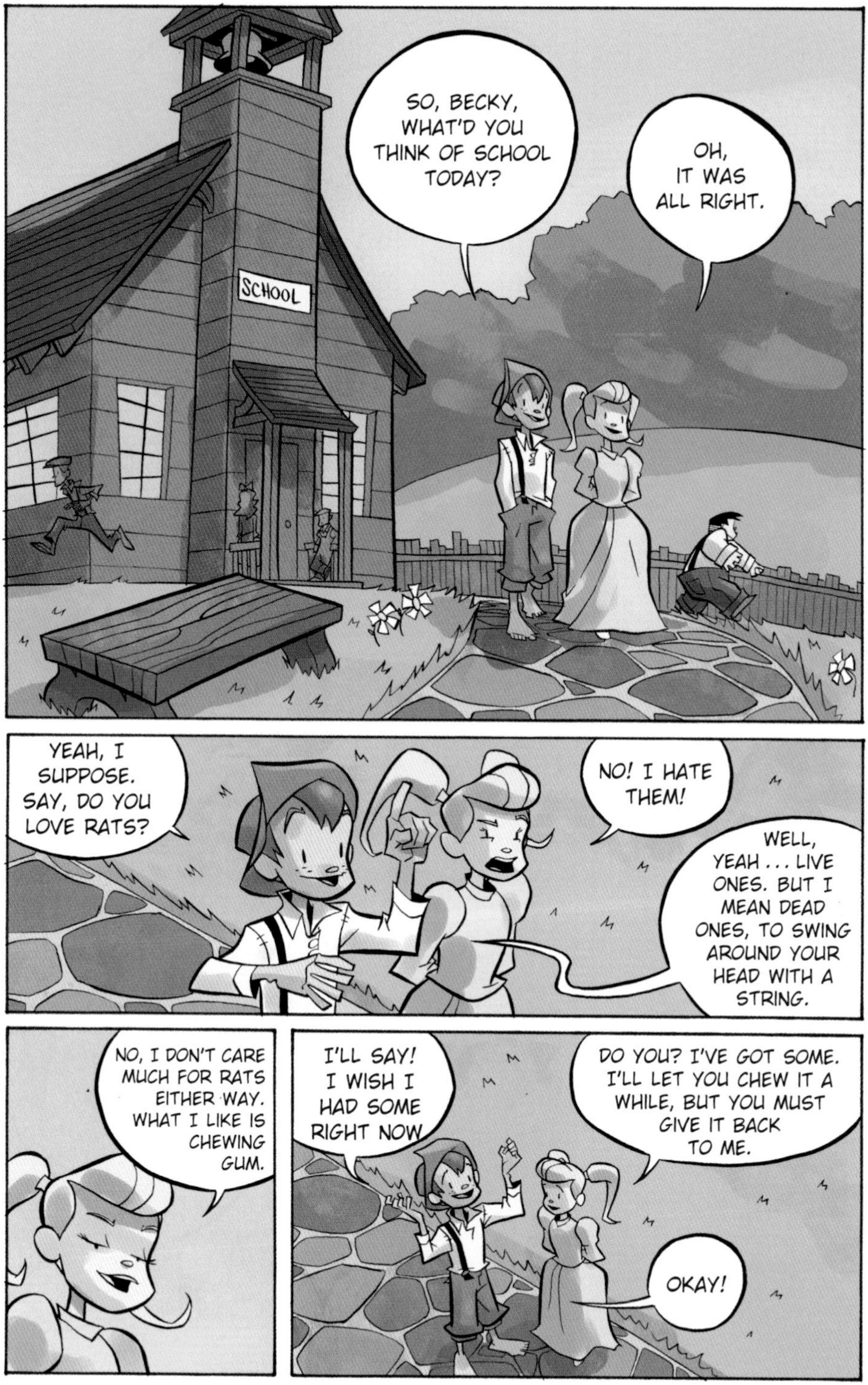
SCHOOL
SO, BECKY, WHAT'D YOU THINK OF SCHOOL TODAY?
OH, IT WAS ALL RIGHT.
YEAH, I SUPPOSE. SAY, DO YOU LOVE RATS?
NO! I HATE THEM!
WELL, YEAH . . . LIVE ONES. BUT I MEAN DEAD ONES, TO SWING AROUND YOUR HEAD WITH A STRING.
NO, I DON'T CARE MUCH FOR RATS EITHER WAY. WHAT I LIKE IS CHEWING GUM.
I'LL SAY! I WISH I HAD SOME RIGHT NOW.
DO YOU? I'VE GOT SOME. I'LL LET YOU CHEW IT A WHILE, BUT YOU MUST GIVE IT BACK TO ME.
OKAY!

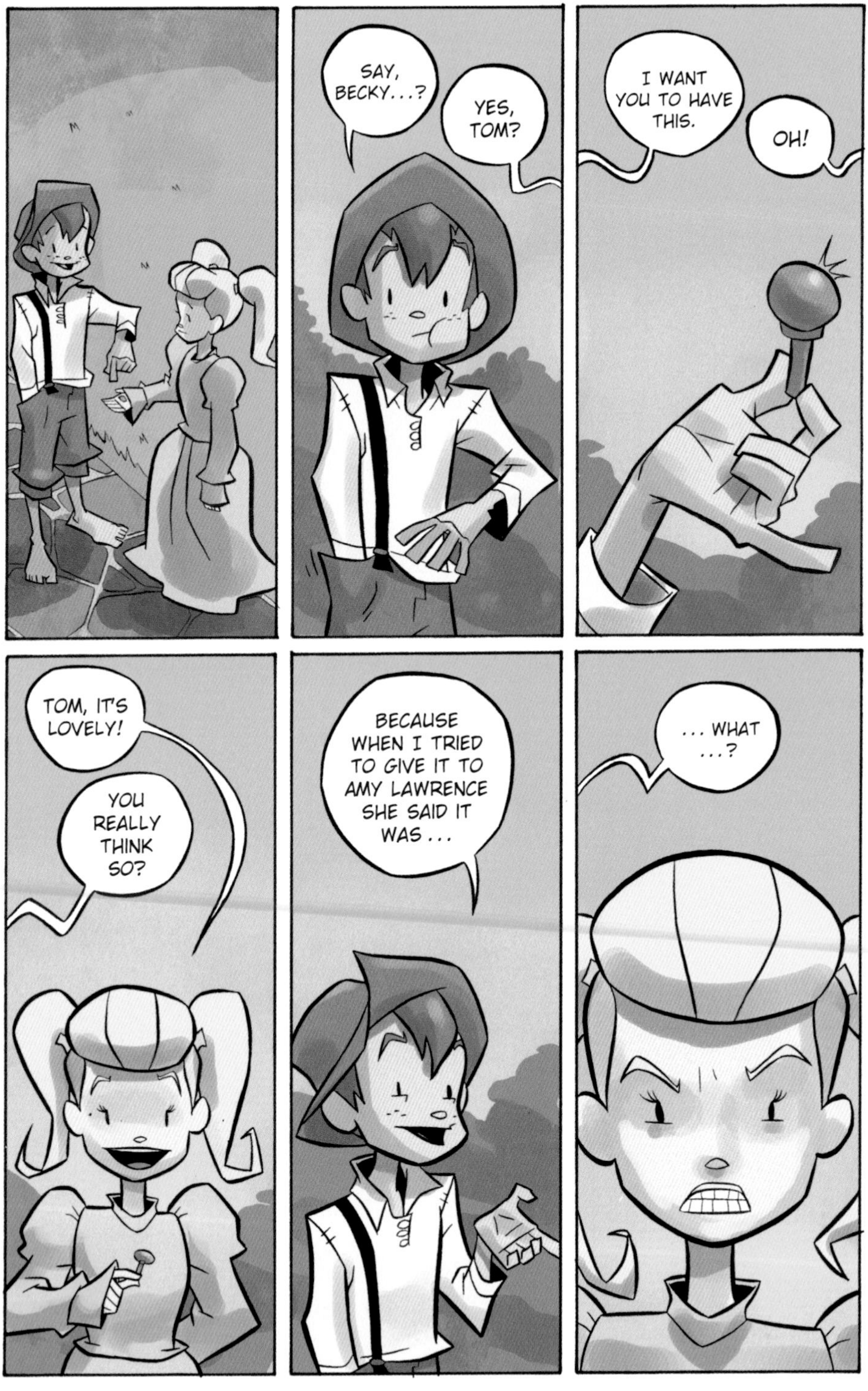
SAY, BECKY...?
YES, TOM?
I WANT YOU TO HAVE THIS.
OH!
TOM, IT'S LOVELY!
YOU REALLY THINK SO?
BECAUSE WHEN I TRIED TO GIVE IT TO AMY LAWRENCE SHE SAID IT WAS ...
... WHAT ...?

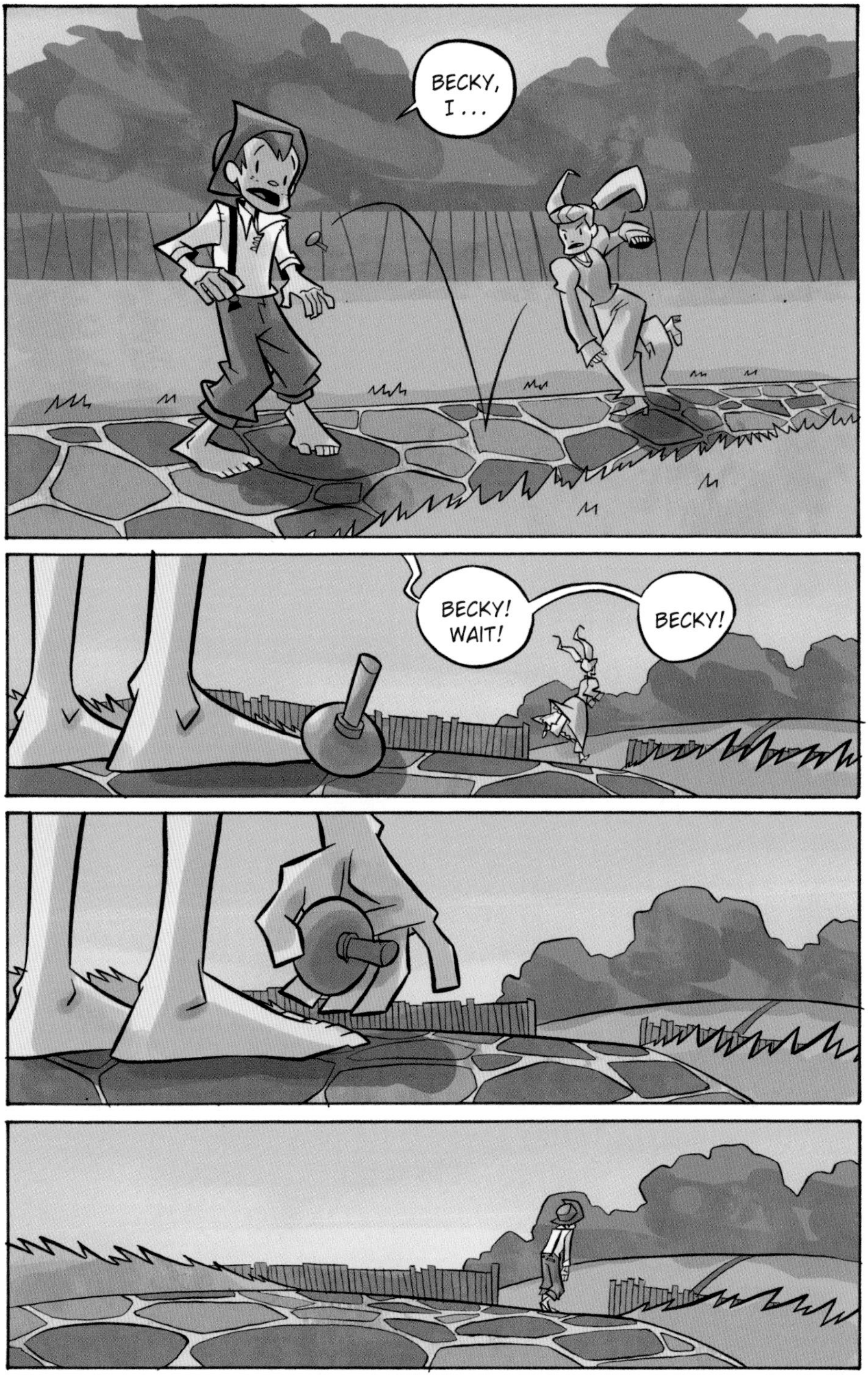
BECKY, I...
BECKY! WAIT!
BECKY!

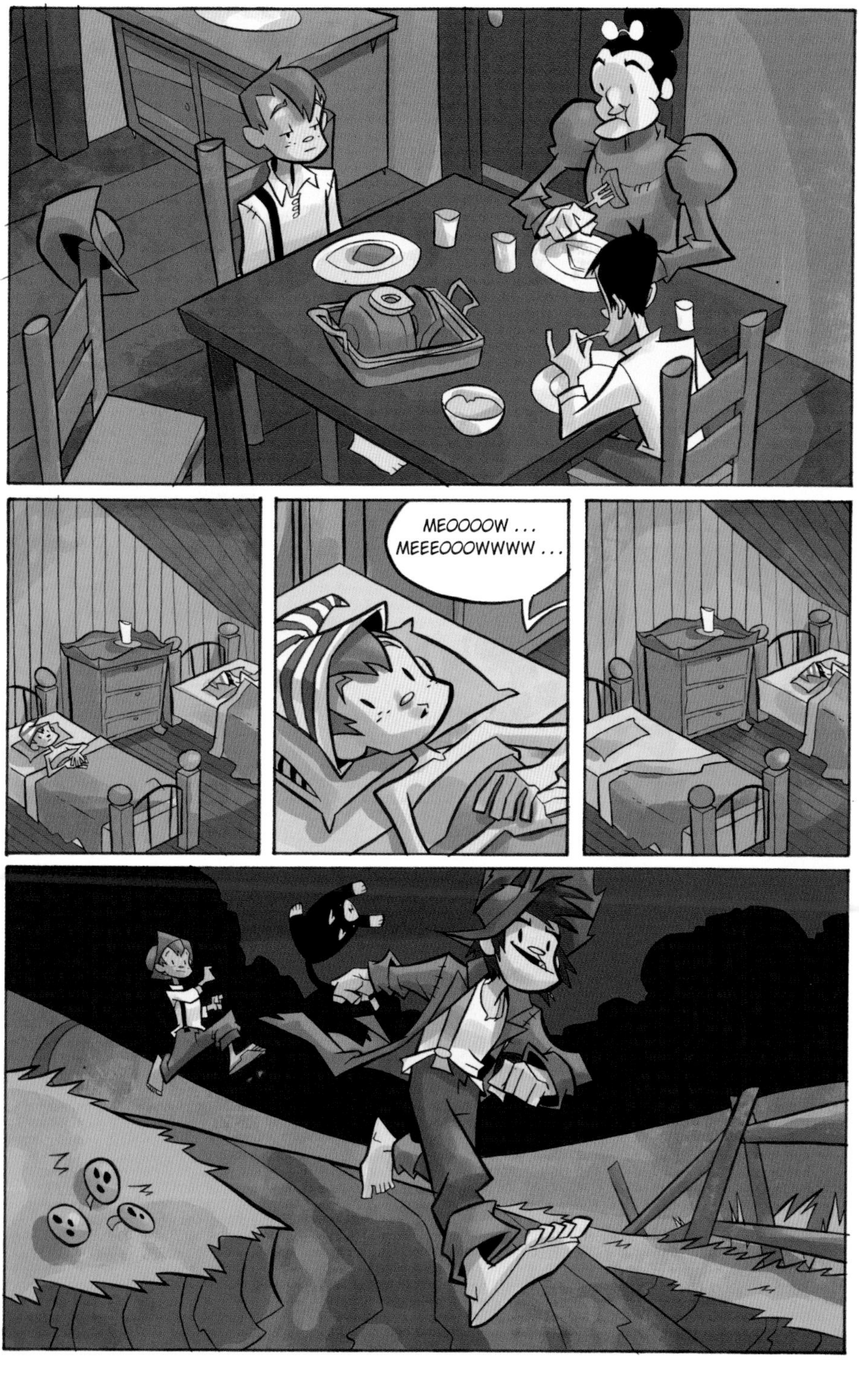
MEOOOOW . . .
MEEEOOOWWWW . . .

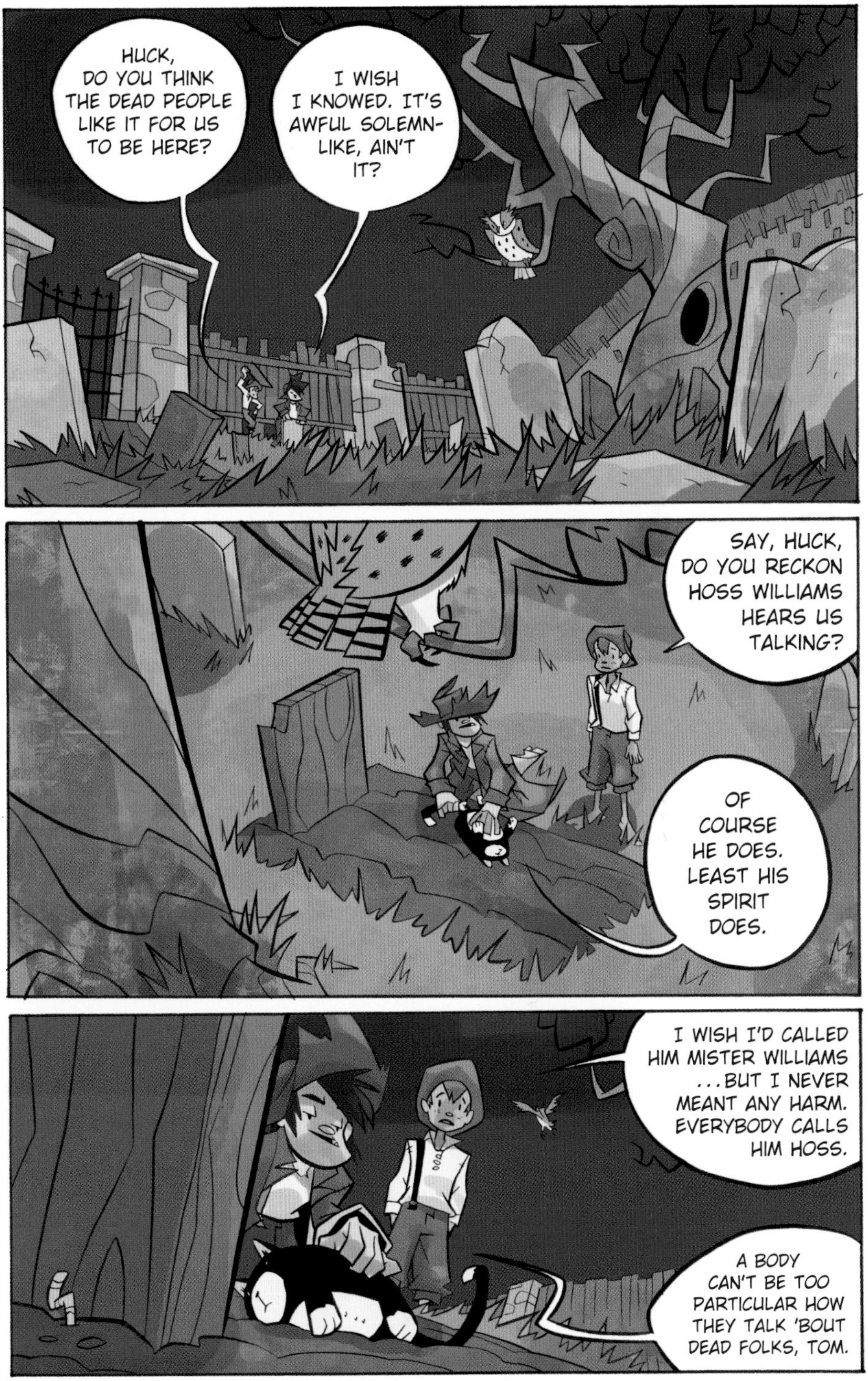
HUCK, DO YOU THINK THE DEAD PEOPLE LIKE IT FOR US TO BE HERE?
I WISH I KNOWED. IT'S AWFUL SOLEMN-LIKE, AIN'T IT?
SAY, HUCK, DO YOU RECKON HOSS WILLIAMS HEARS US TALKING?
OF COURSE HE DOES. LEAST HIS SPIRIT DOES.
I WISH I'D CALLED HIM MISTER WILLIAMS . . . BUT I NEVER MEANT ANY HARM. EVERYBODY CALLS HIM HOSS.
A BODY CAN'T BE TOO PARTICULAR HOW THEY TALK 'BOUT DEAD FOLKS, TOM.

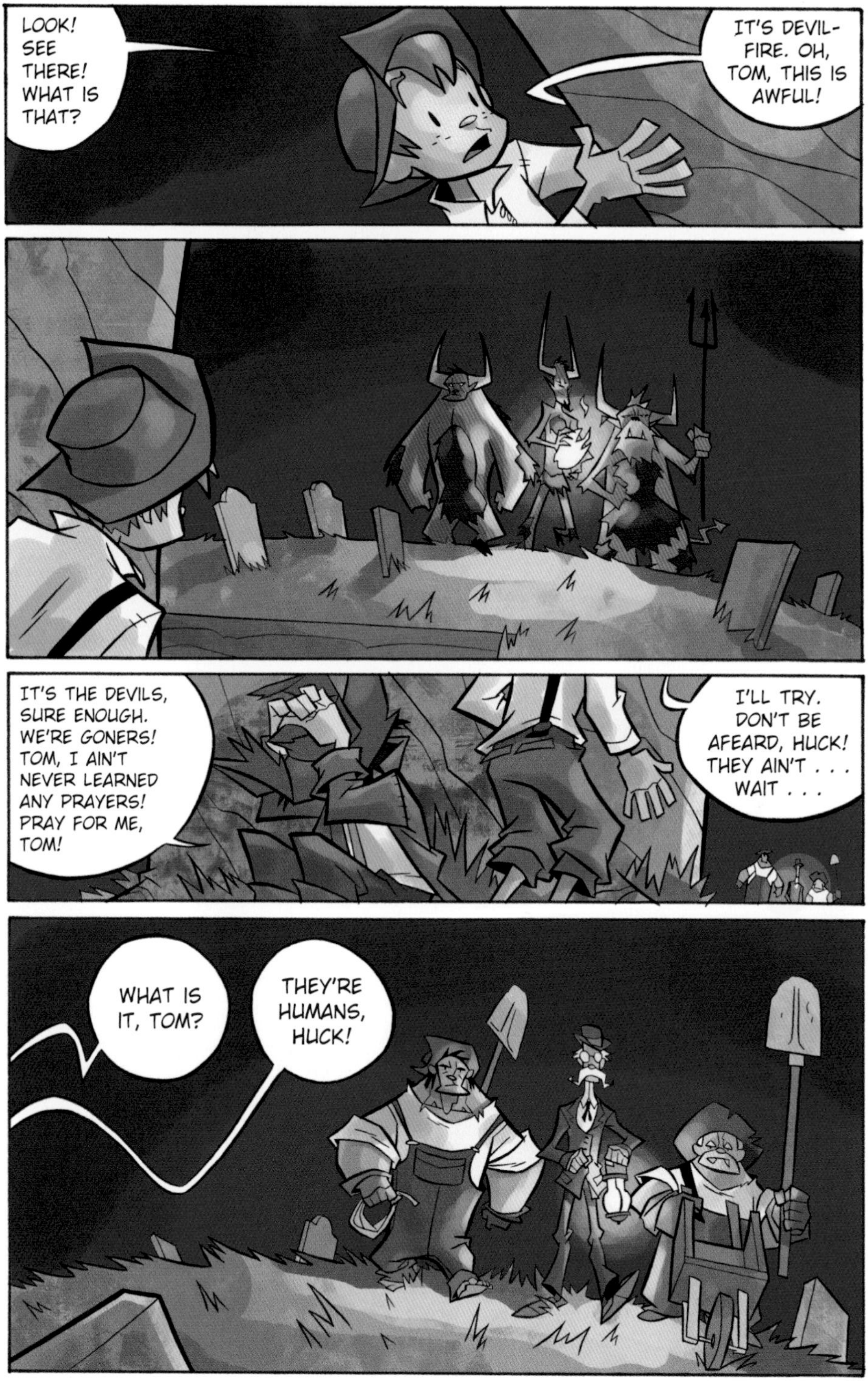
LOOK! SEE THERE! WHAT IS THAT?
IT'S DEVIL-FIRE. OH, TOM, THIS IS AWFUL!
IT'S THE DEVILS, SURE ENOUGH. WE'RE GONERS! TOM, I AIN'T NEVER LEARNED ANY PRAYERS! PRAY FOR ME, TOM!
I'LL TRY. DON'T BE AFEARD, HUCK! THEY AIN'T . . . WAIT . . .
WHAT IS IT, TOM?
THEY'RE HUMANS, HUCK!

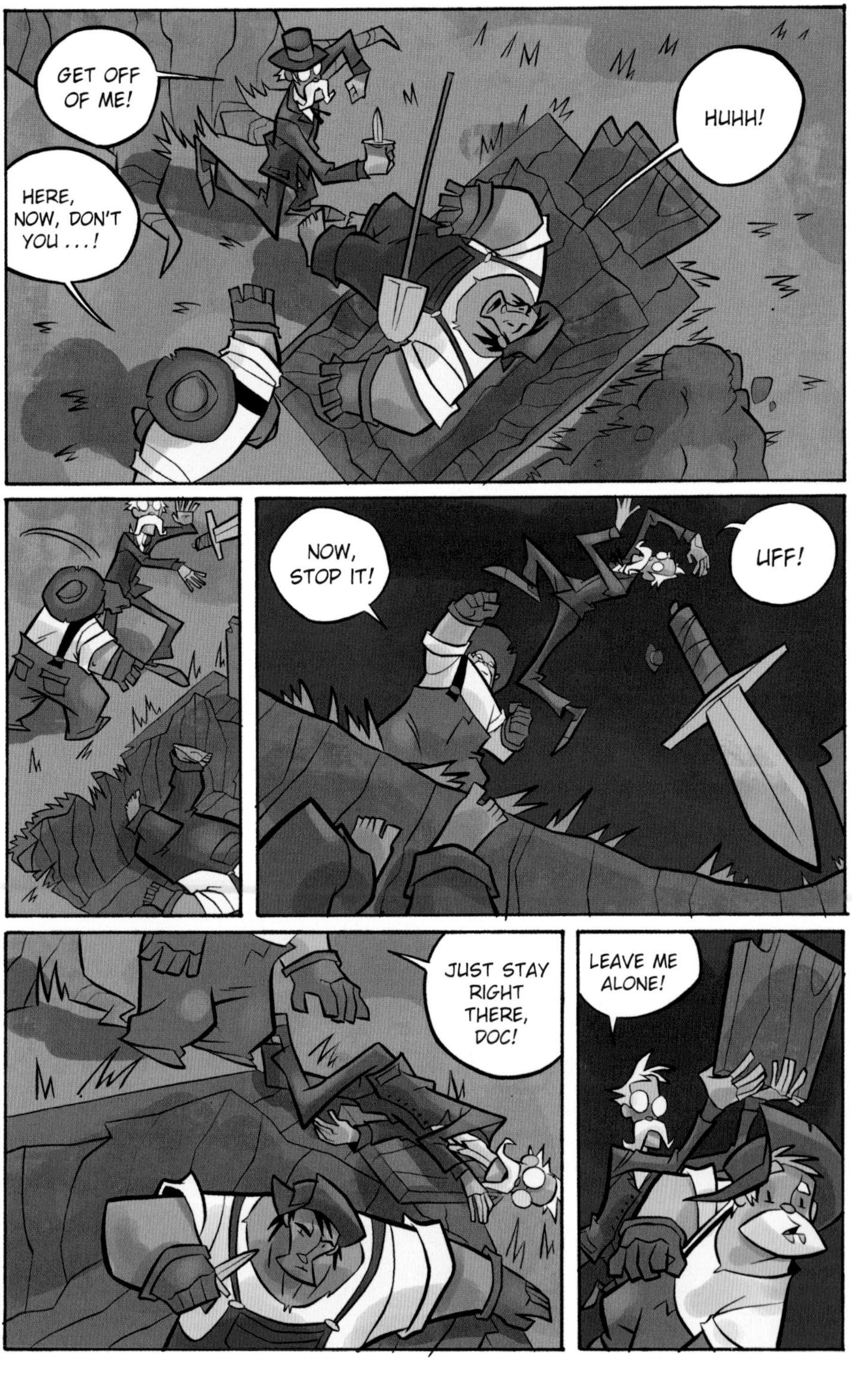
GET OFF OF ME!
HERE, NOW, DON'T YOU . . .!
HUHH!
NOW, STOP IT!
UFF!
JUST STAY RIGHT THERE, DOC!
LEAVE ME ALONE!

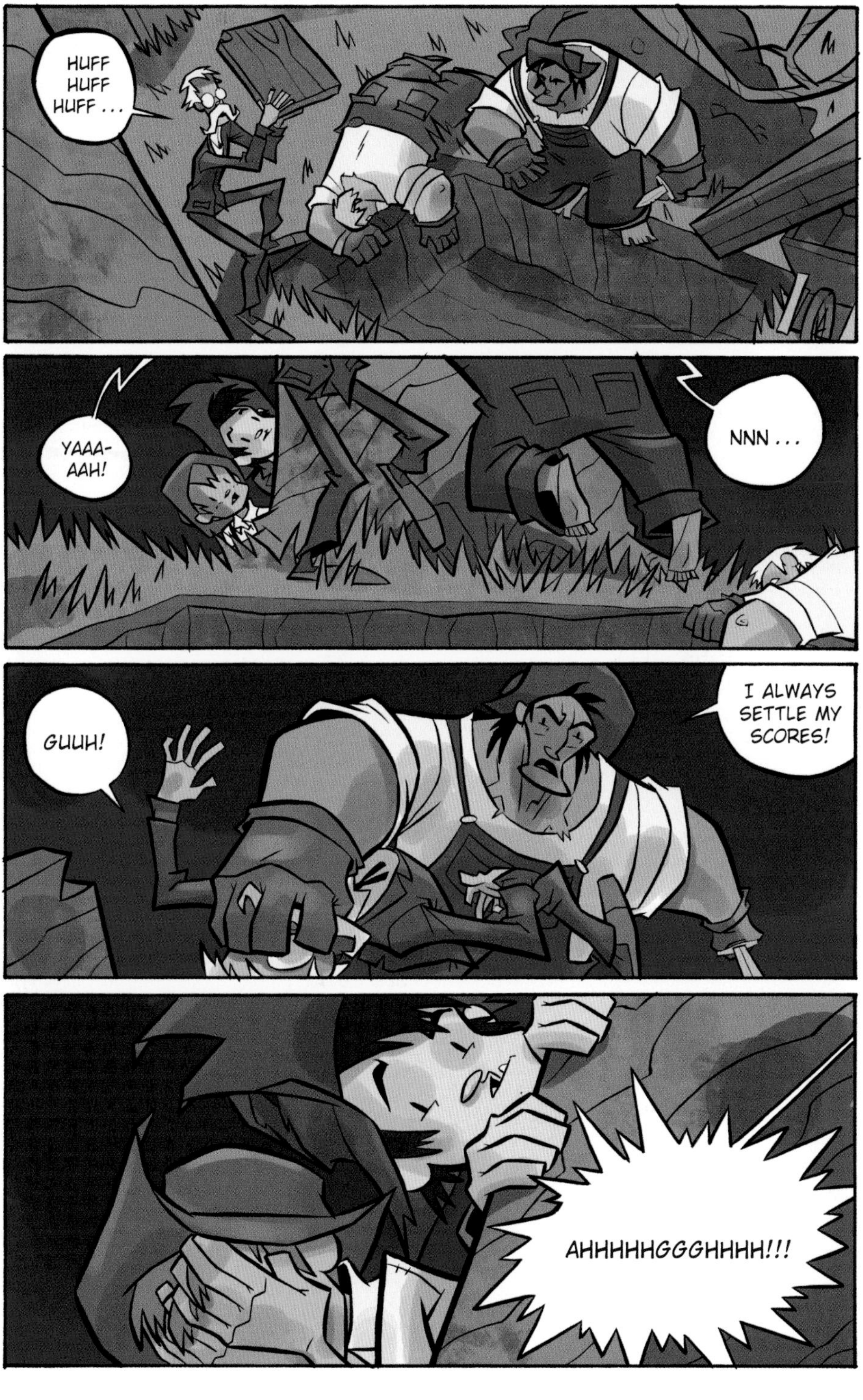
HUFF
HUFF
HUFF . . .
YAAA-
AAH!
NNN . . .
GUUH!
I ALWAYS
SETTLE MY
SCORES!
AHHHHHGGGHHHH!!!

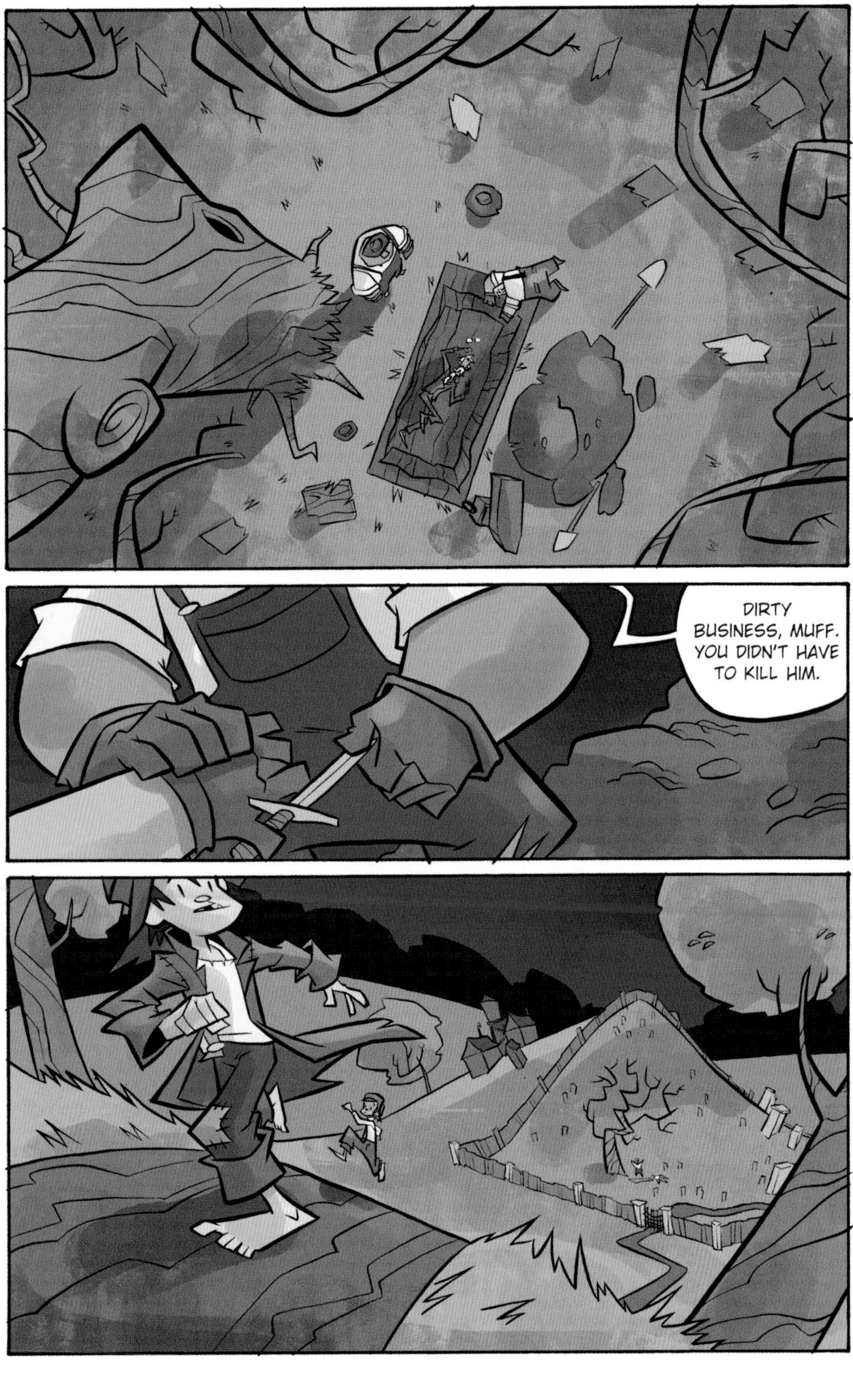
DIRTY BUSINESS, MUFF. YOU DIDN'T HAVE TO KILL HIM.

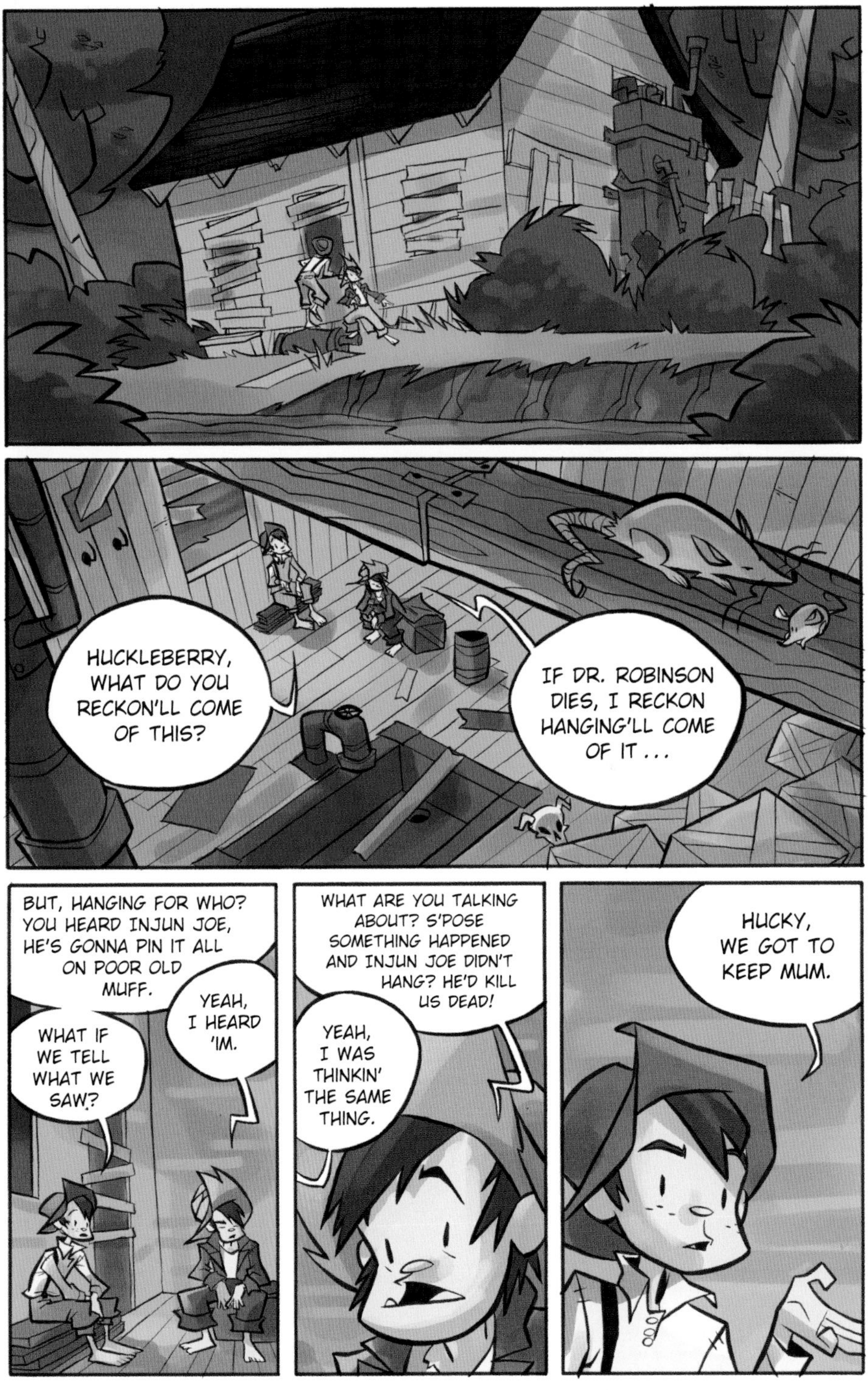
HUCKLEBERRY, WHAT DO YOU RECKON'LL COME OF THIS?
IF DR. ROBINSON DIES, I RECKON HANGING'LL COME OF IT . . .
BUT, HANGING FOR WHO? YOU HEARD INJUN JOE, HE'S GONNA PIN IT ALL ON POOR OLD MUFF.
YEAH, I HEARD 'IM.
WHAT IF WE TELL WHAT WE SAW?
WHAT ARE YOU TALKING ABOUT? S'POSE SOMETHING HAPPENED AND INJUN JOE DIDN'T HANG? HE'D KILL US DEAD!
YEAH, I WAS THINKIN' THE SAME THING.
HUCKY, WE GOT TO KEEP MUM.

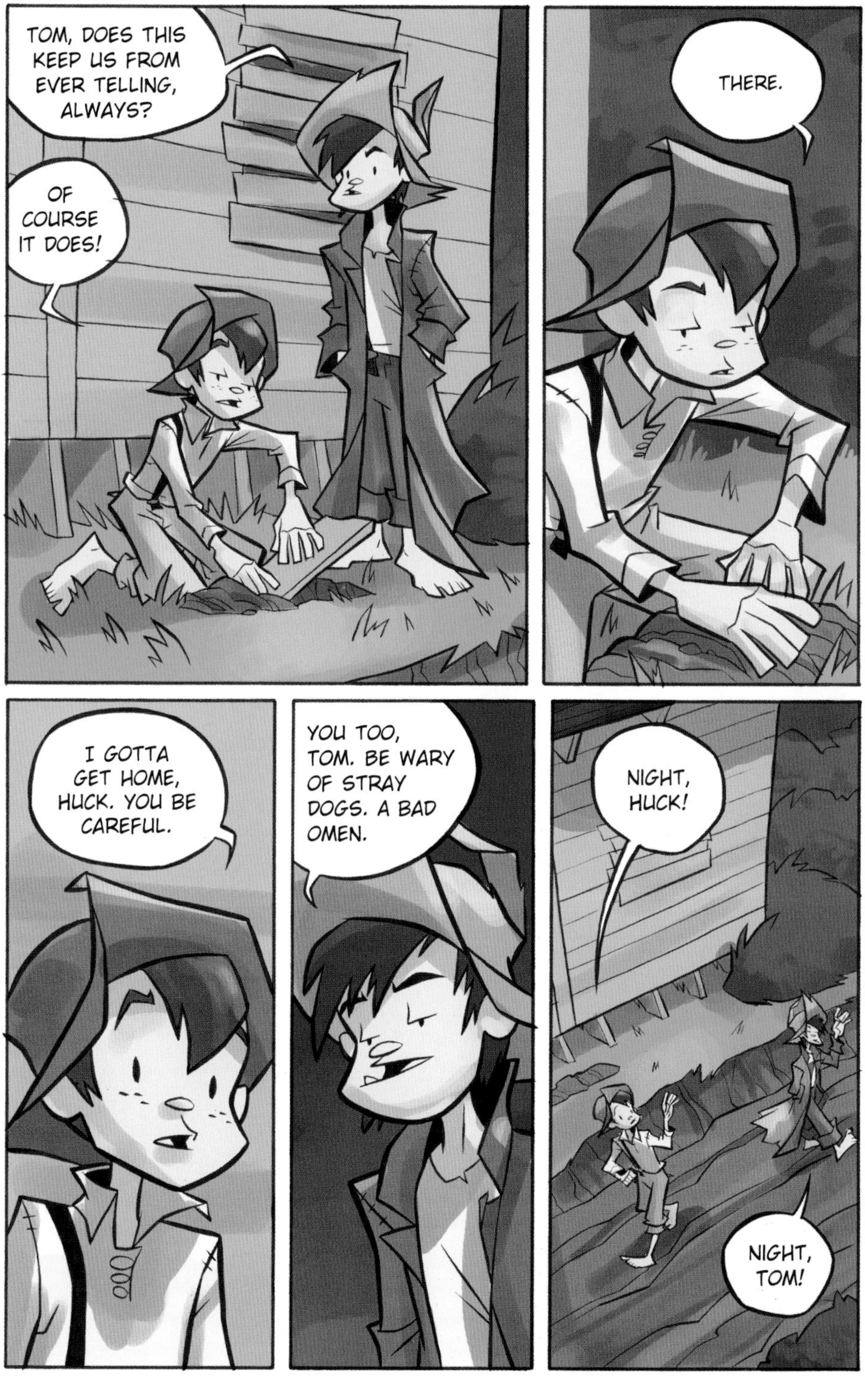
TOM, DOES THIS KEEP US FROM EVER TELLING, ALWAYS?
OF COURSE IT DOES!
THERE.
I GOTTA GET HOME, HUCK. YOU BE CAREFUL.
YOU TOO, TOM. BE WARY OF STRAY DOGS. A BAD OMEN.
NIGHT, HUCK!
NIGHT, TOM!

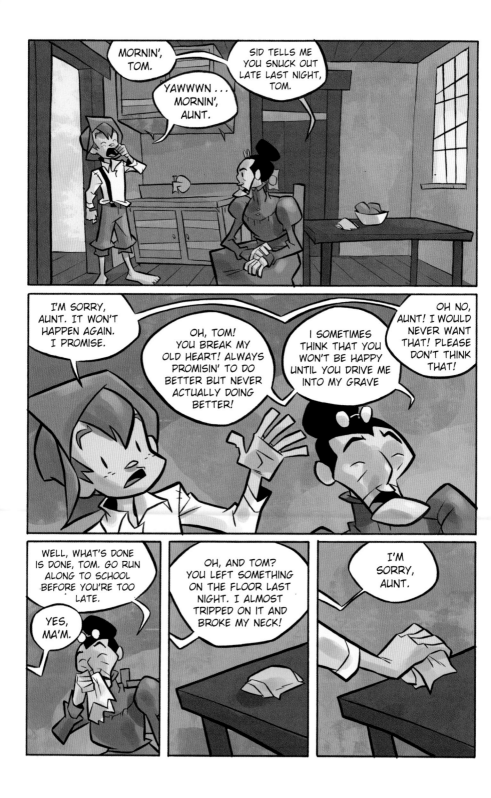

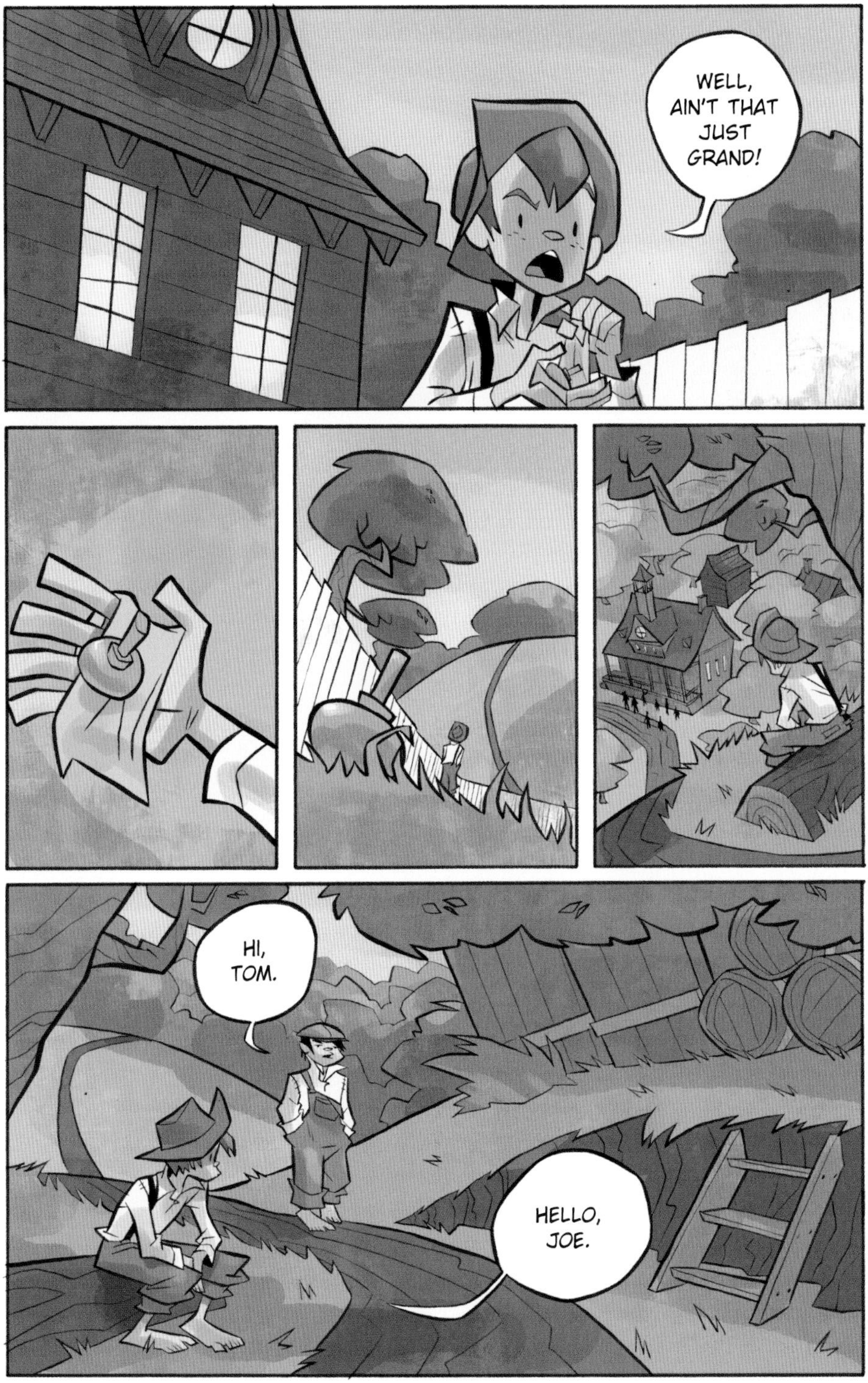
WELL, AIN'T THAT JUST GRAND!
HI, TOM.
HELLO, JOE.

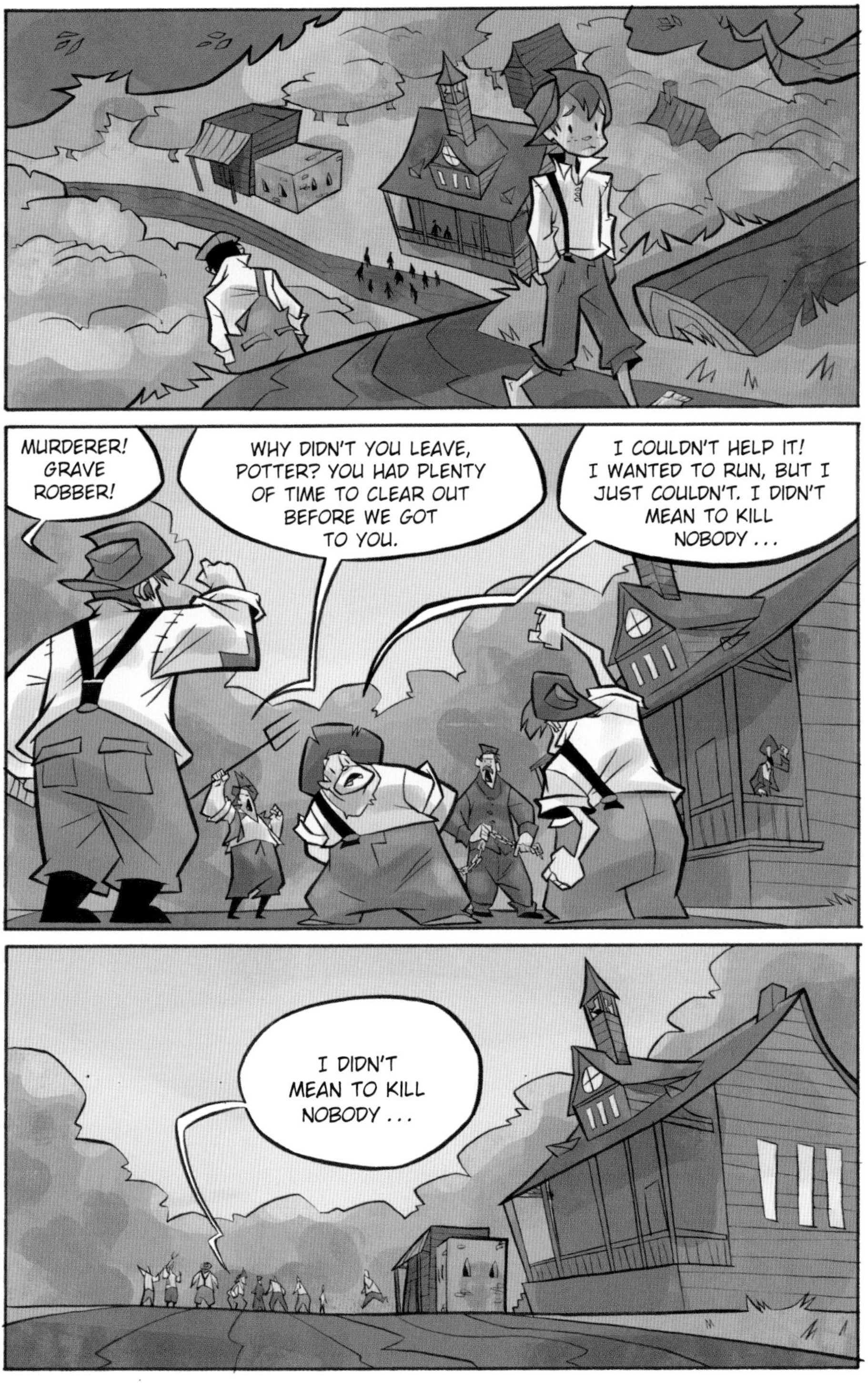
MURDERER! GRAVE ROBBER!
WHY DIDN'T YOU LEAVE, POTTER? YOU HAD PLENTY OF TIME TO CLEAR OUT BEFORE WE GOT TO YOU.
I COULDN'T HELP IT! I WANTED TO RUN, BUT I JUST COULDN'T. I DIDN'T MEAN TO KILL NOBODY . . .
I DIDN'T MEAN TO KILL NOBODY . . .

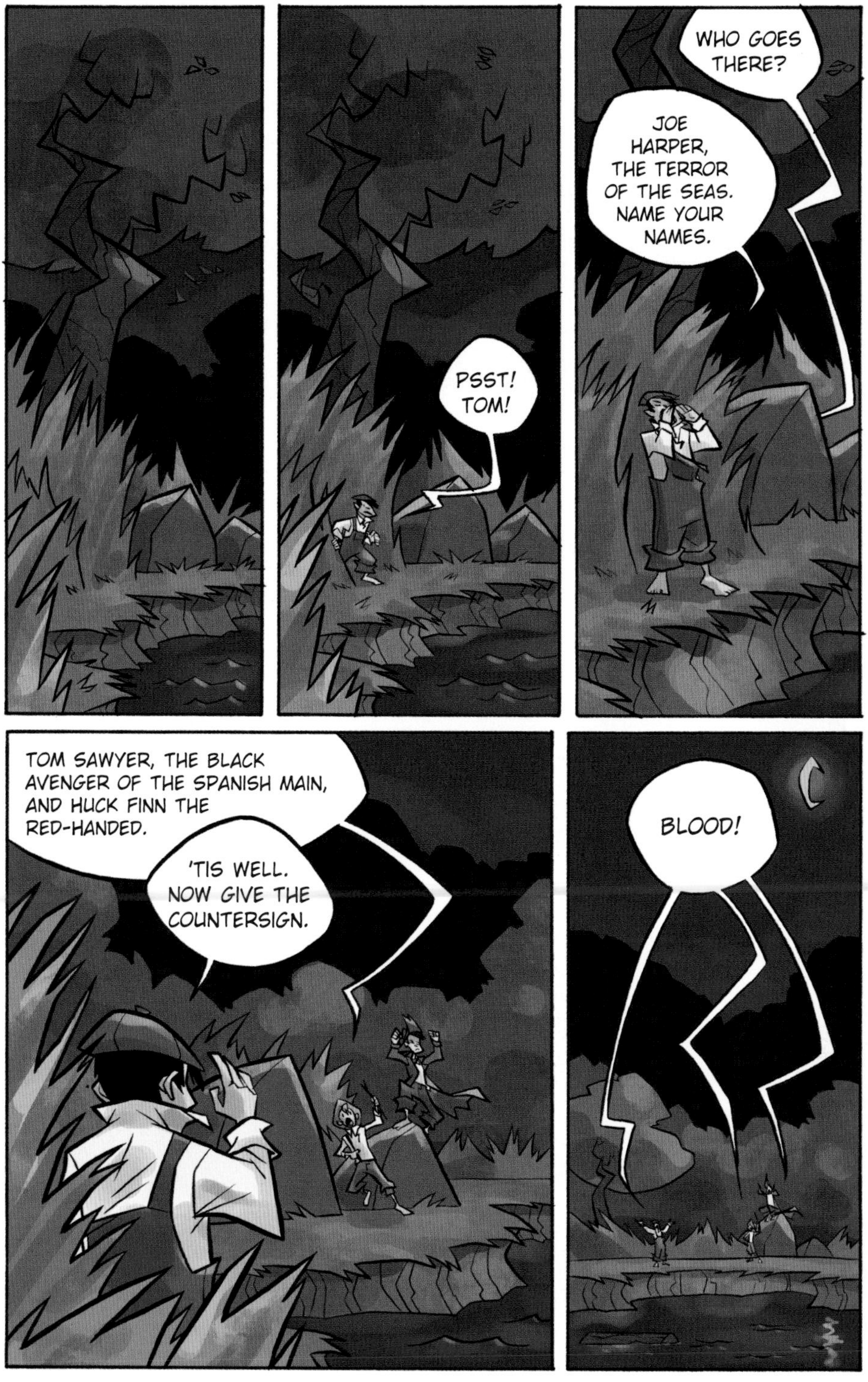
PSST! TOM!
WHO GOES THERE?
JOE HARPER, THE TERROR OF THE SEAS. NAME YOUR NAMES.
TOM SAWYER, THE BLACK AVENGER OF THE SPANISH MAIN, AND HUCK FINN THE RED-HANDED.
'TIS WELL. NOW GIVE THE COUNTERSIGN.
BLOOD!

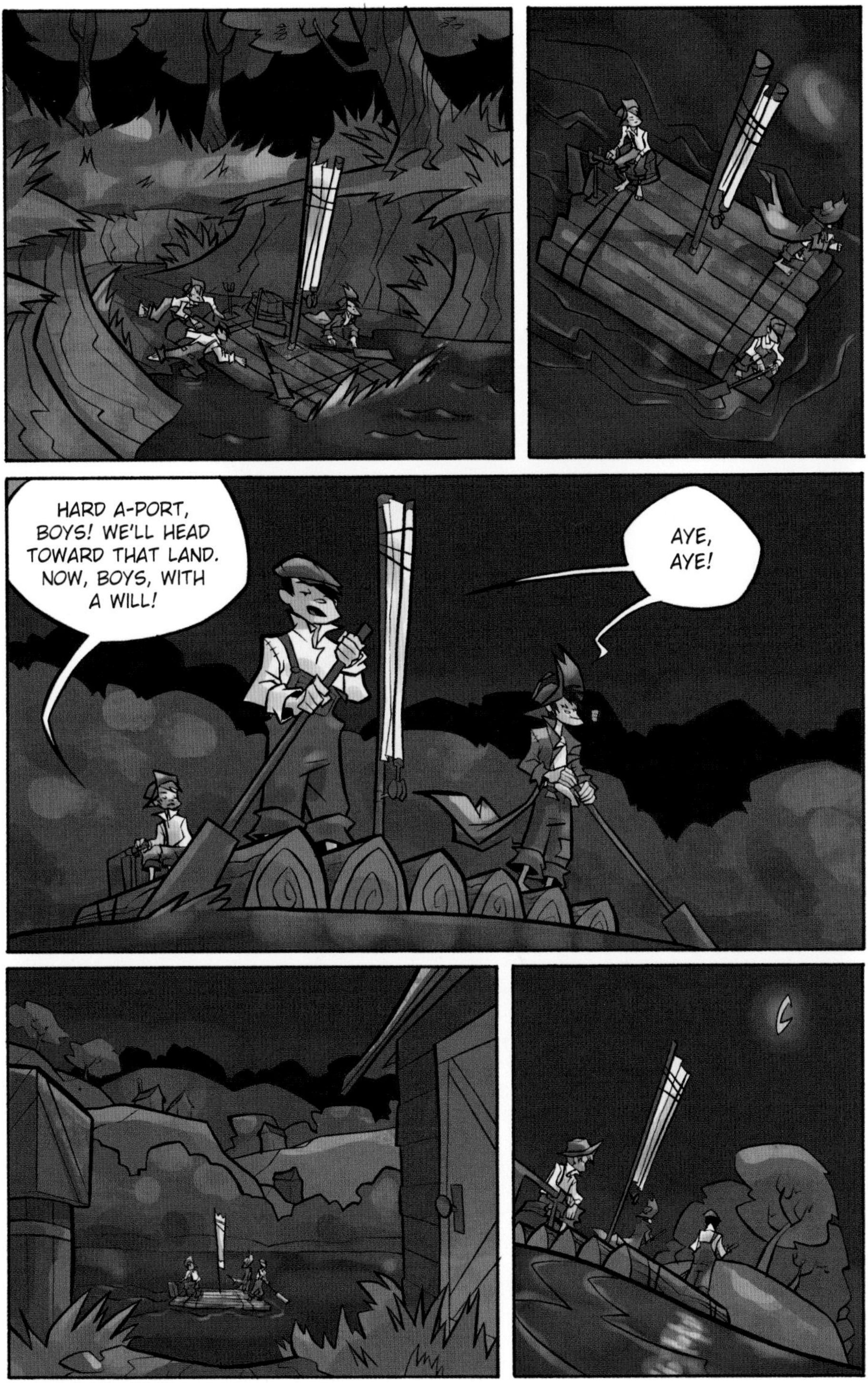
HARD A-PORT, BOYS! WE'LL HEAD TOWARD THAT LAND. NOW, BOYS, WITH A WILL!
AYE, AYE!

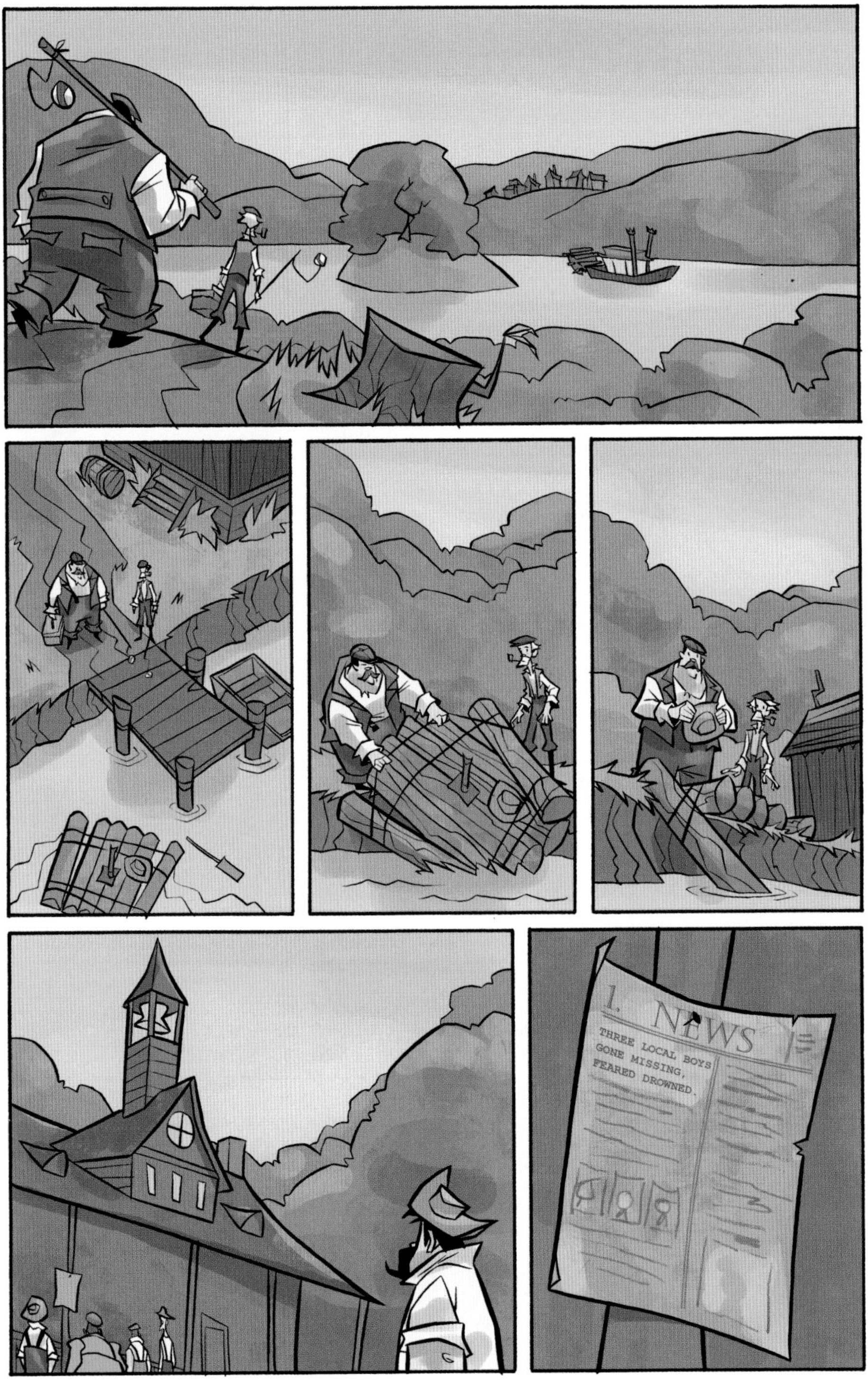
1.
NEWS
THREE LOCAL BOYS GONE MISSING, FEARED DROWNED.

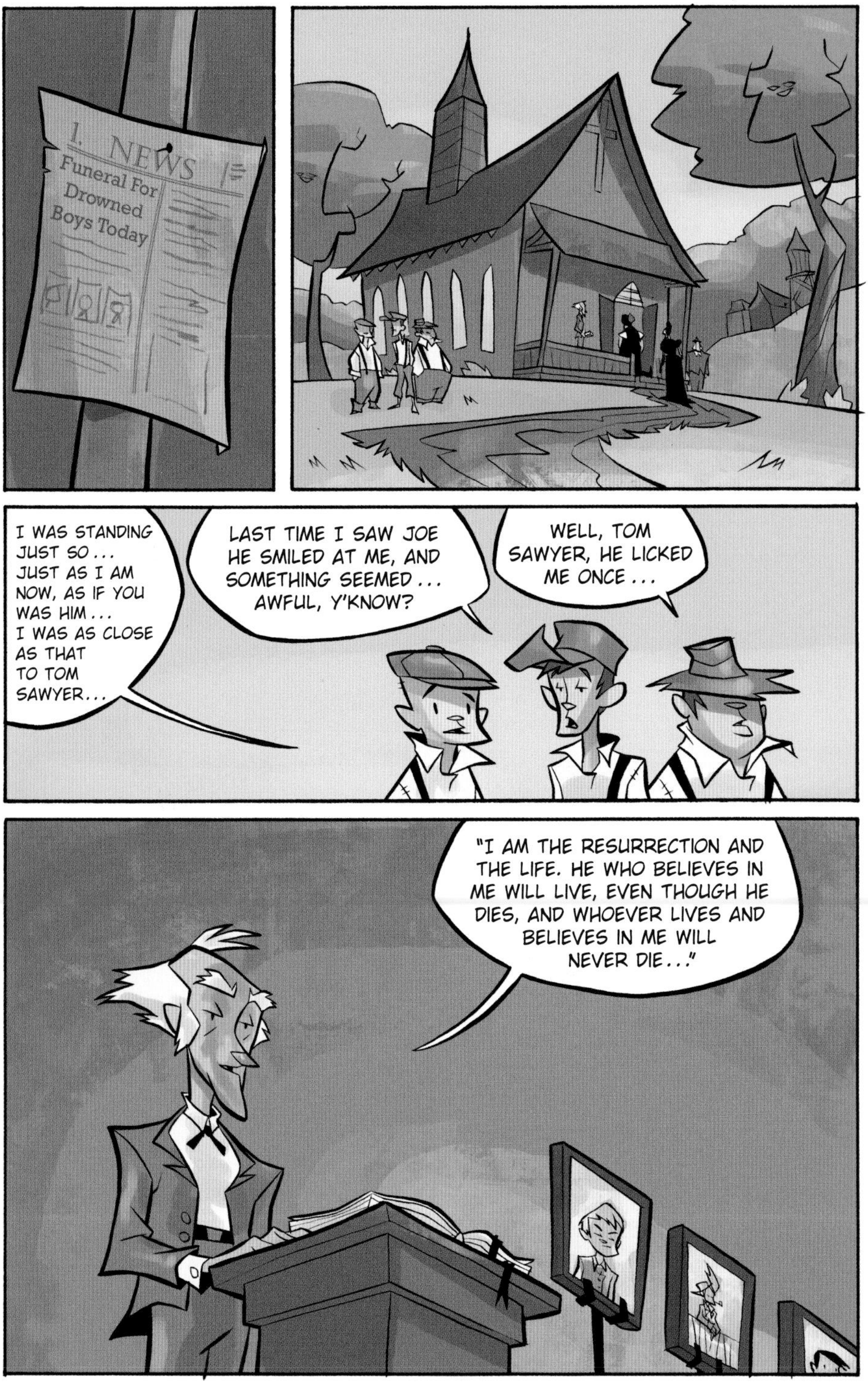
1. NEWS
Funeral For Drowned Boys Today
I WAS STANDING JUST SO . . . JUST AS I AM NOW, AS IF YOU WAS HIM . . . I WAS AS CLOSE AS THAT TO TOM SAWYER . . .
LAST TIME I SAW JOE HE SMILED AT ME, AND SOMETHING SEEMED . . . AWFUL, Y'KNOW?
WELL, TOM SAWYER, HE LICKED ME ONCE . . .
"I AM THE RESURRECTION AND THE LIFE. HE WHO BELIEVES IN ME WILL LIVE, EVEN THOUGH HE DIES, AND WHOEVER LIVES AND BELIEVES IN ME WILL NEVER DIE . . ."

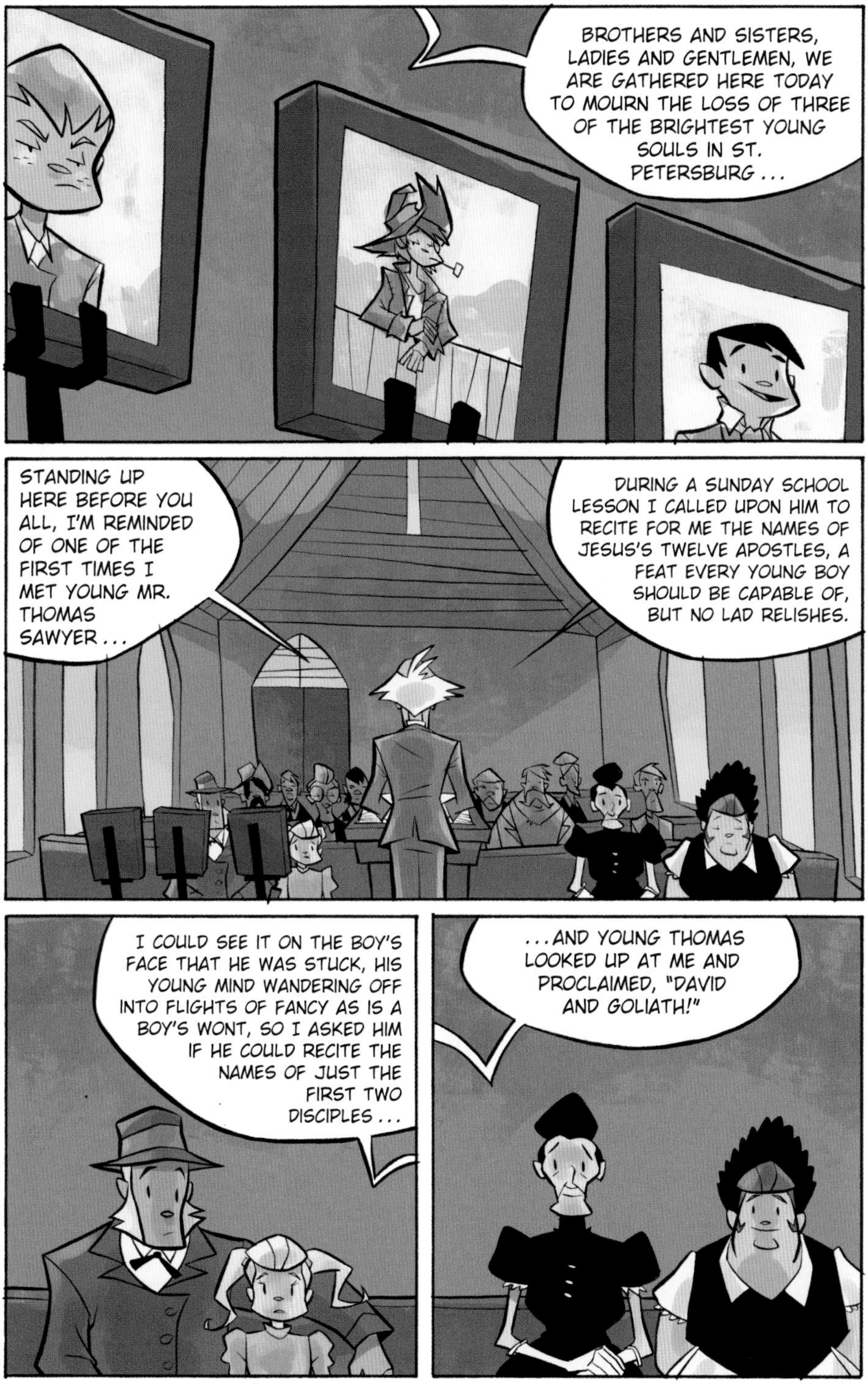
BROTHERS AND SISTERS, LADIES AND GENTLEMEN, WE ARE GATHERED HERE TODAY TO MOURN THE LOSS OF THREE OF THE BRIGHTEST YOUNG SOULS IN ST. PETERSBURG . . .
STANDING UP HERE BEFORE YOU ALL, I'M REMINDED OF ONE OF THE FIRST TIMES I MET YOUNG MR. THOMAS SAWYER . . .
DURING A SUNDAY SCHOOL LESSON I CALLED UPON HIM TO RECITE FOR ME THE NAMES OF JESUS'S TWELVE APOSTLES, A FEAT EVERY YOUNG BOY SHOULD BE CAPABLE OF, BUT NO LAD RELISHES.
I COULD SEE IT ON THE BOY'S FACE THAT HE WAS STUCK, HIS YOUNG MIND WANDERING OFF INTO FLIGHTS OF FANCY AS IS A BOY'S WONT, SO I ASKED HIM IF HE COULD RECITE THE NAMES OF JUST THE FIRST TWO DISCIPLES . . .
. . . AND YOUNG THOMAS LOOKED UP AT ME AND PROCLAIMED, "DAVID AND GOLIATH!"

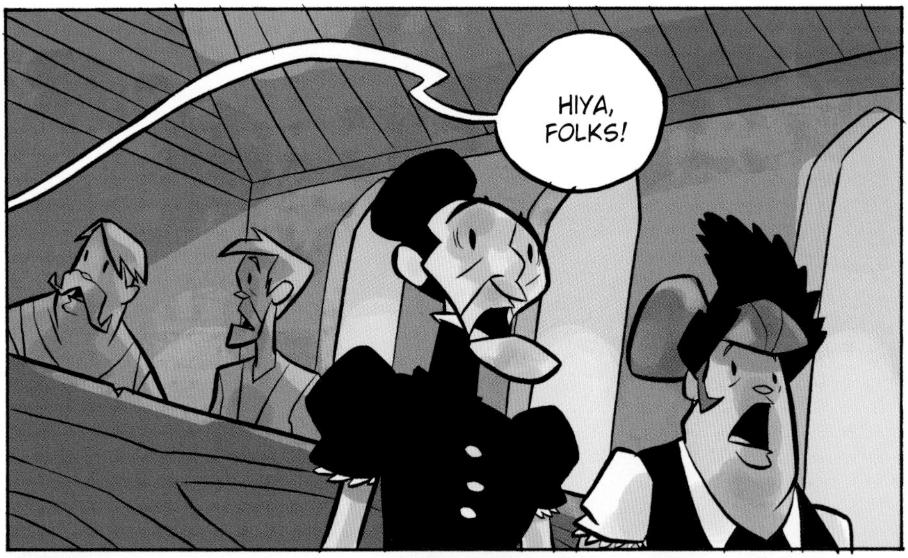
HIYA, FOLKS!

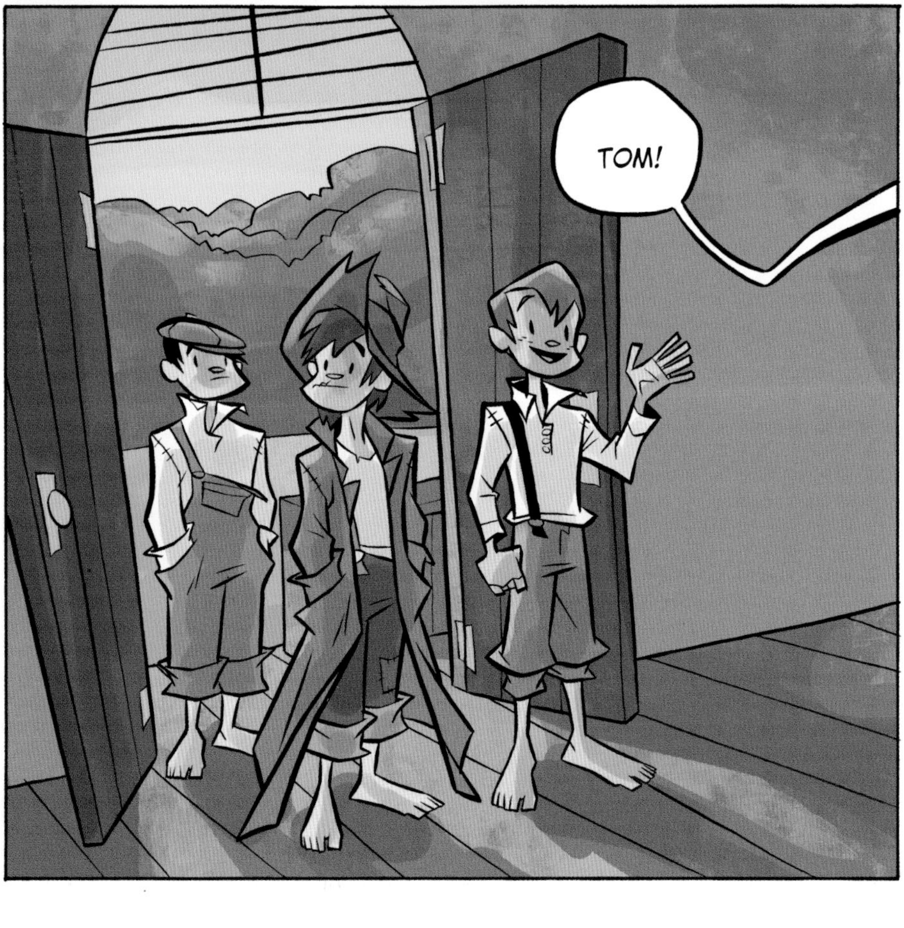
TOM!

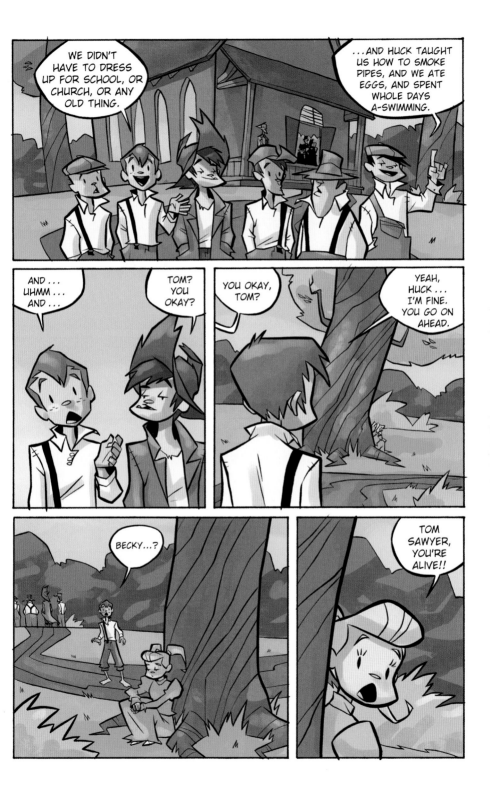

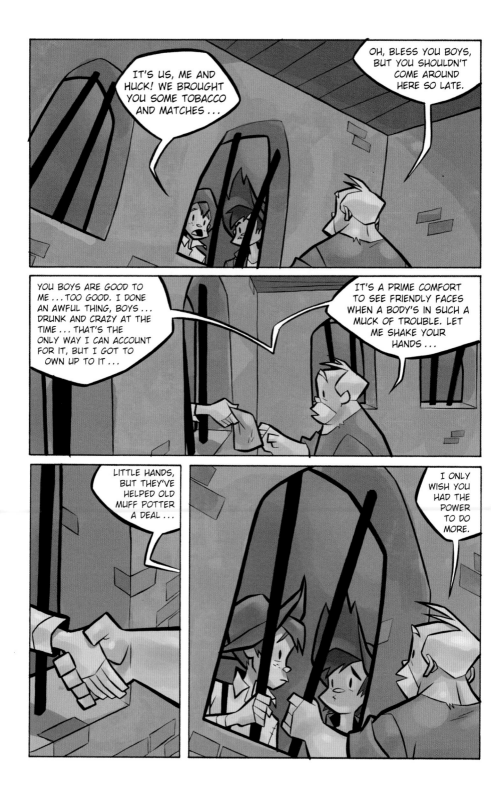

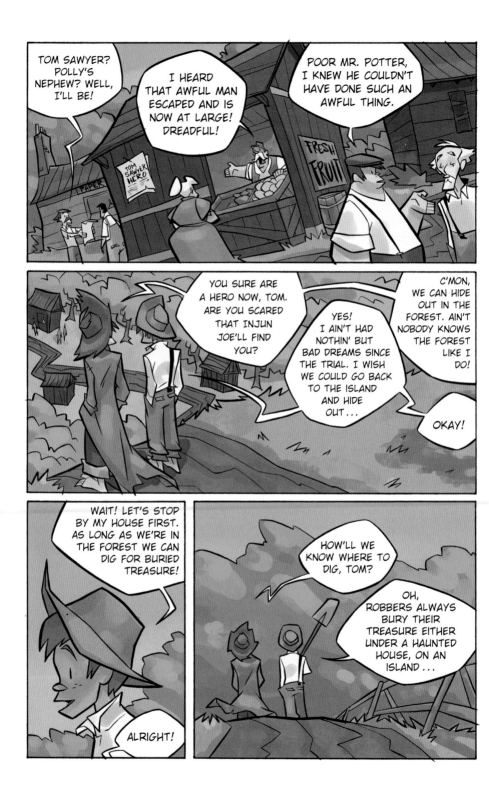

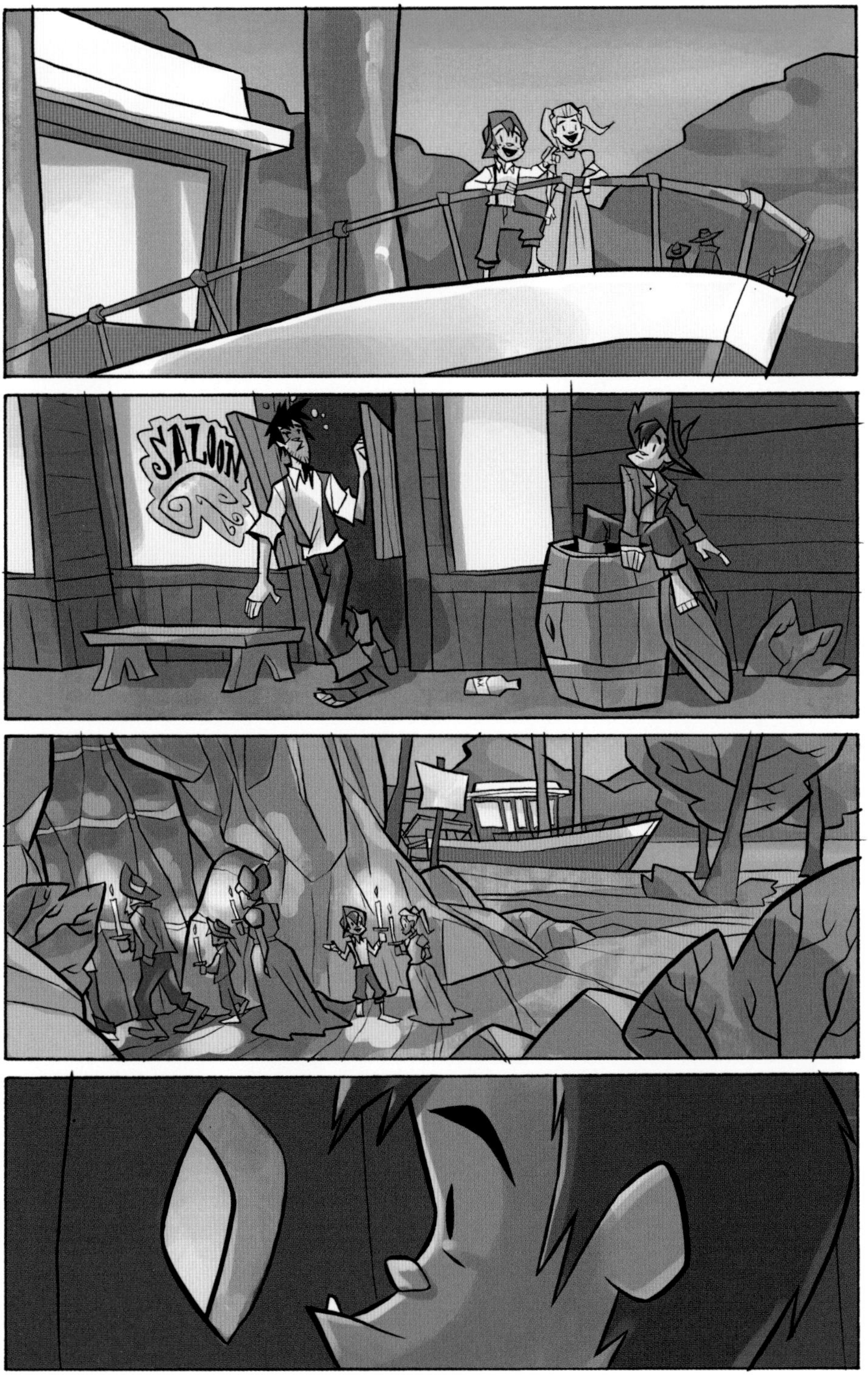
SALOON

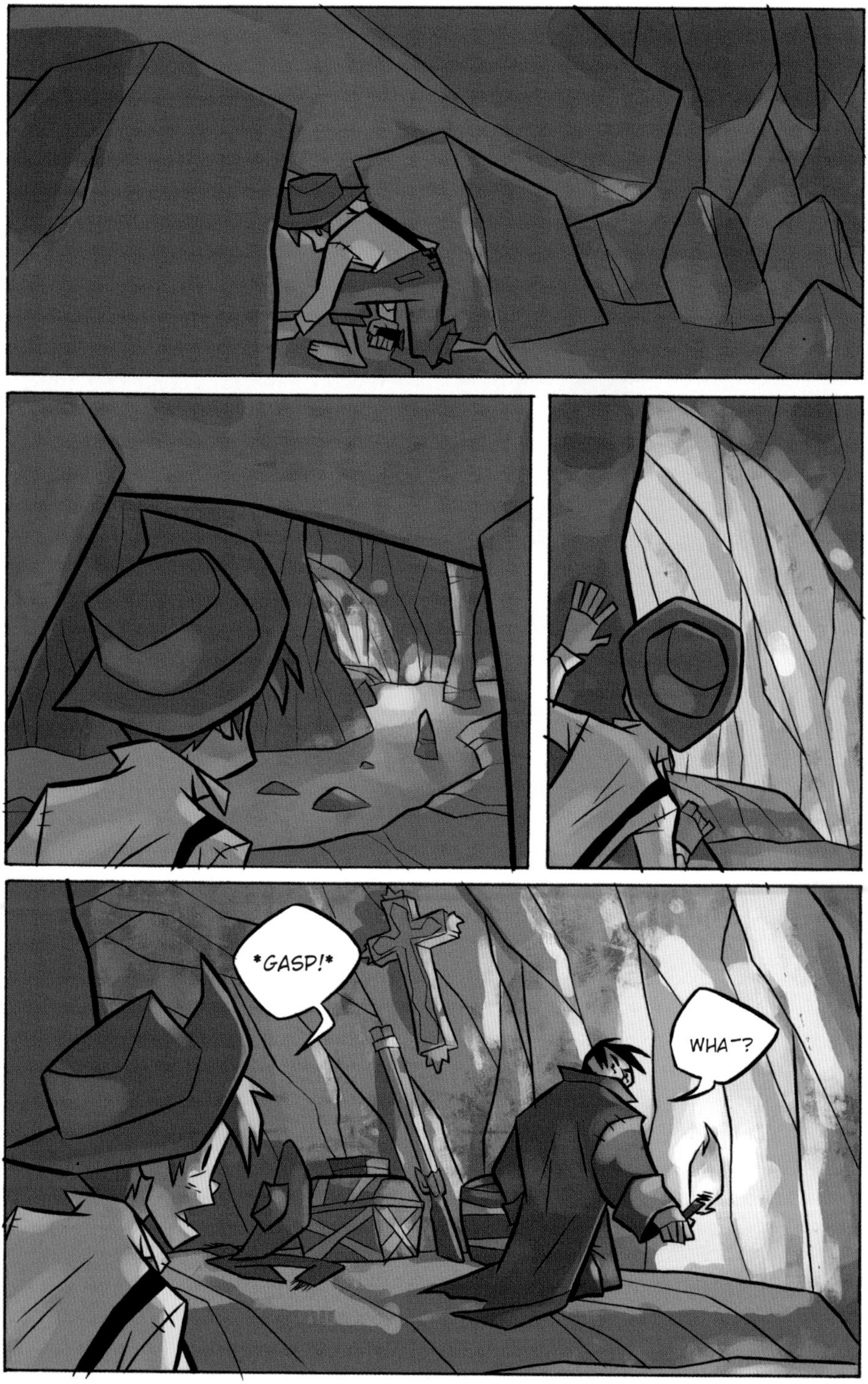
GASP!
WHA–?

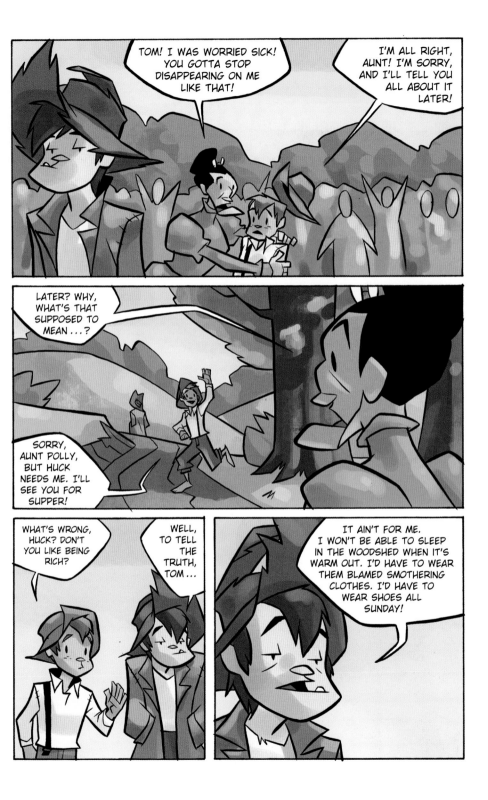

ABOUT MARK TWAIN

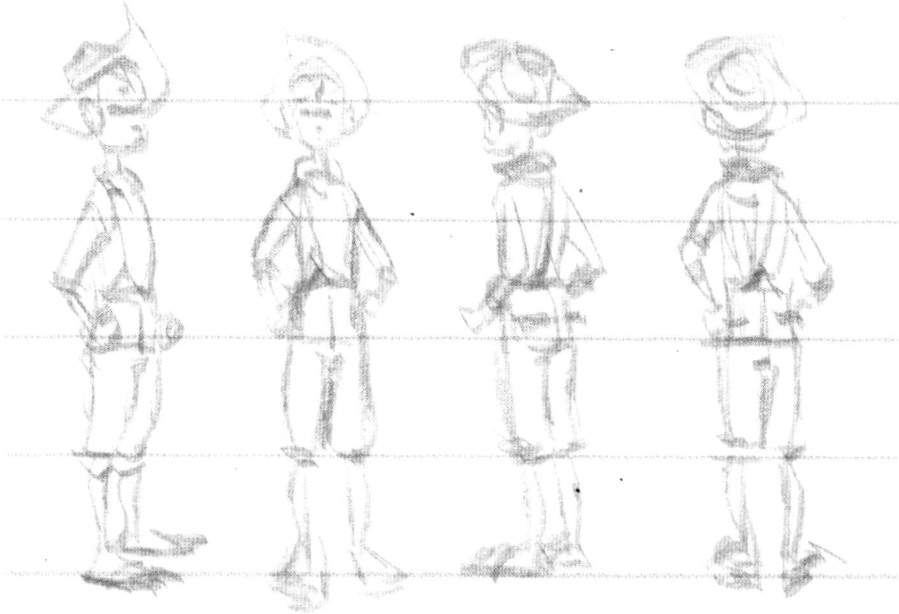

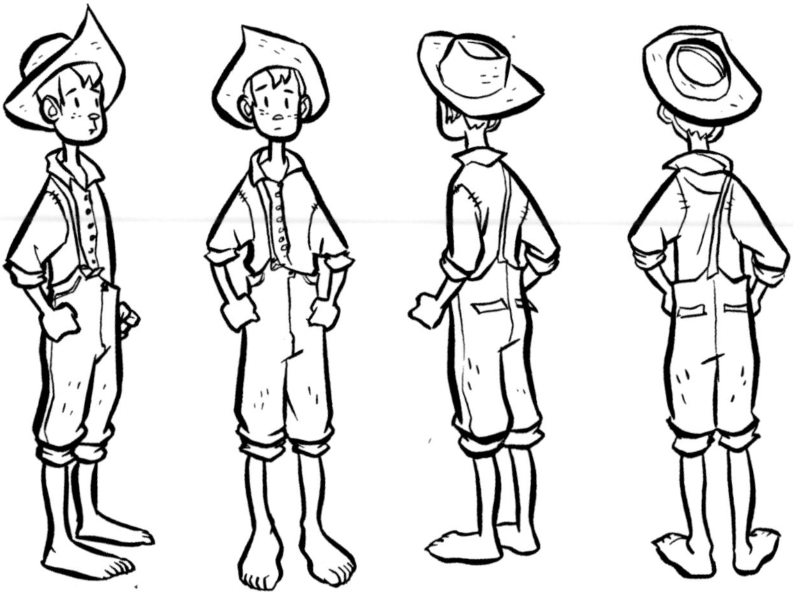

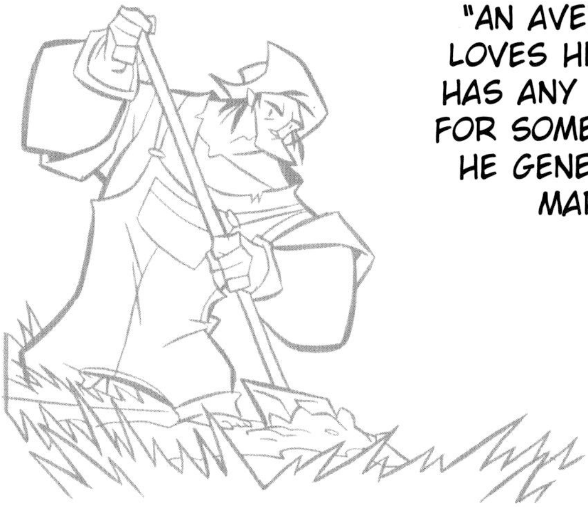

"AN AVERAGE AMERICAN LOVES HIS FAMILY. IF HE HAS ANY LOVE LEFT OVER FOR SOME OTHER PERSON, HE GENERALLY SELECTS MARK TWAIN."

–THOMAS EDISON

MARK TWAIN IS THE WELL-KNOWN PSEUDONYM OF AMERICAN WRITER, HUMORIST, NOVELIST, AND LECTURER SAMUEL LANGHORNE CLEMENS, BORN THE SIXTH OF SEVEN CHILDREN ON NOVEMBER 30, 1835 IN FLORIDA, MISSOURI. CLEMENS' FAMILY THEN MOVED TO THE PORT TOWN OF HANNIBAL WHEN HE WAS FOUR.

DURING HIS EARLY TEENS, HE WORKED AS AN APPRENTICE PRINTER, HAVING LEFT SCHOOL AFTER COMPLETING FIFTH GRADE. AT SIXTEEN, HE BEGAN WRITING HUMOROUS ARTICLES AND NEWSPAPER SKETCHES. BY THE AGE OF EIGHTEEN, CLEMENS HAD LEFT HANNIBAL TO WORK AS A PRINTER IN NEW YORK, PHILADELPHIA, ST. LOUIS, AND CINCINNATI.

AT THE AGE OF 22, CLEMENS RETURNED TO MISSOURI AND WORKED THERE AS A RIVER-BOAT PILOT–THE LIKELY ORIGIN OF HIS FAMOUS PEN NAME "MARK TWAIN. "TWO FATHOMS (12 FT), THE NAUTICAL TERM FOR "SAFE WATER," WAS MEASURED WITH A SOUNDING LINE, AND MARKED BY CALLING OUT "MARK TWAIN." TWAIN HIMSELF NEVER CONFIRMED THE SOURCE OF HIS PEN NAME. CLEMENS CONTINUED TO WORK AS A RIVER BOAT PILOT UNTIL 1861, WHEN THE AMERICAN CIVIL WAR BEGAN.

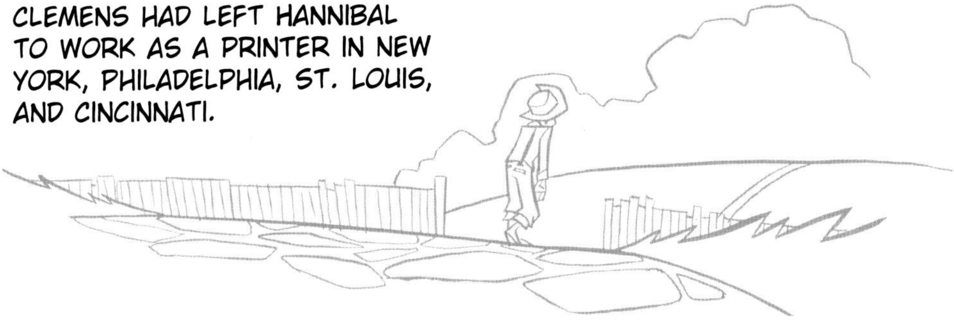

AFTER FAILING AS A SILVER PROSPECTOR, CLEMENS OBTAINED WORK AT A NEWSPAPER IN VIRGINIA CITY CALLED THE "DAILY TERRITORIAL ENTERPRISE," AND ADOPTED THE NAME MARK TWAIN.

BY 1864, TWAIN HEADED TO SAN FRANCISCO TO WRITE FOR THE LOCAL PAPERS. A YEAR LATER HE WAS SENT TO REPORT ON THE SANDWICH ISLANDS IN HAWAII. HIS TRAVEL WRITINGS WERE SO POPULAR THAT, ON HIS RETURN, HE BEGAN A SERIES OF FAMOUS LECTURE TOURS, CEMENTING HIS POPULARITY AS A PUBLIC SPEAKER AND STAGE PRESENCE.

AT THE START OF THE CIVIL WAR, CLEMENS AND HIS FRIENDS FORMED A CONFEDERATE MILITIA CALLED THE MARION RANGERS, WHICH DISBANDED AFTER TWO WEEKS DUE TO LACK OF MILITARY ACTION.

WHILE HIS FRIENDS WENT OFF TO JOIN THE CONFEDERATE ARMY, CLEMENS AND HIS BROTHER, ORION (THE NEWLY APPOINTED SECRETARY TO THE TERRITORIAL GOVERNOR OF NEVADA), HEADED WEST—AN EXPERIENCE THAT CLEMENS CONSIDERED SIGNIFICANT TO HIS FORMATION AS A WRITER AND THAT BECAME THE BASIS FOR A TRAVEL BOOK "ROUGHING IT." SAMUEL AND ORION TRAVELED BY STAGECOACH, AND EXPERIENCED A VARIETY OF MISADVENTURES, INCLUDING THEIR FIRST ENCOUNTER WITH NATIVE AMERICAN TRIBES.

TWAIN HAD BECOME THE MOST POPULAR AMERICAN CELEBRITY OF HIS AGE. HIS FAMOUS FRIENDS INCLUDED INVENTOR, PHYSICIST AND MECHANICAL ENGINEER NIKOLA TESLA; DEAF AND BLIND AUTHOR/ACTIVIST HELEN KELLER; AND AUTHOR ROBERT LOUIS STEVENSON. BY 1873 TWAIN HAD SETTLED DOWN WITH HIS WIFE, OLIVIA, IN A 19-ROOM FARMHOUSE IN HARTFORD, CONNECTICUT, AND IT WAS FROM 1874 TO 1891 THAT TWAIN COMPLETED HIS MOST FAMOUS WORKS. IN 1876 TWAIN PUBLISHED ONE OF HIS MOST ENDEARING NOVELS, "TOM SAWYER."

IN "TOM SAWYER," TWAIN CAPTURED HIS OWN CHILDHOOD MEMORIES OF GROWING UP IN HANNIBAL, MISSOURI, AND BASED MANY OF THE CHARACTERS ON PEOPLE HE KNEW AS A CHILD. TOM, FOR INSTANCE, IS A COMPOSITE OF TWAIN'S CHILDHOOD FRIENDS JOHN BRIGGS AND WILL BOWEN, AND OF HIMSELF. JANE CLEMENS, TWAIN'S MOTHER, WAS HIS MODEL FOR AUNT POLLY, AND HIS BROTHER HENRY WAS THE BASIS FOR SID, THOUGH TWAIN ADMITS THAT HENRY WAS "A MUCH FINER AND BETTER BOY THAN SID EVER WAS."

"NEVER PUT OFF UNTIL TOMORROW THAT WHICH COULD BE DONE THE DAY AFTER TOMORROW."

–MARK TWAIN

"IN WRITING 'TOM SAWYER' I HAD NO IDEA OF LAYING DOWN RULES FOR THE BRINGING UP OF SMALL FAMILIES, BUT MERELY TO THROW OUT HINTS AS TO HOW THEY MIGHT BRING THEMSELVES UP, AND THE BOYS SEEMED TO HAVE CAUGHT THE IDEA NICELY."

—MARK TWAIN

HUCK WAS MODELED AFTER AN "IGNORANT, UNWASHED, AND INSUFFICIENTLY FED" BOY NAMED TOM BLANKENSHIP. BECKY THATCHER HAS HER ROOTS IN LAURA HAWKINS, A GIRL WHO LIVED ACROSS THE STREET FROM TWAIN AND WHO HE HAD A CRUSH ON. THERE WAS ALSO A REAL INJUN JOE, BUT IT IS LIKELY THAT HE WAS JUST A LOAFER AND A DRUNK, NOT THE ARCH-VILLAIN THAT TWAIN PORTRAYED.

CHILDHOOD INFLUENCES ASIDE, TOM SAWYER AND HUCK FINN ARE ALSO BASED ON TWO FAMOUS LITERARY CHARACTERS; DON QUIXOTE AND SANCHO PANZA FROM CERVANTES' "DON QUIXOTE."

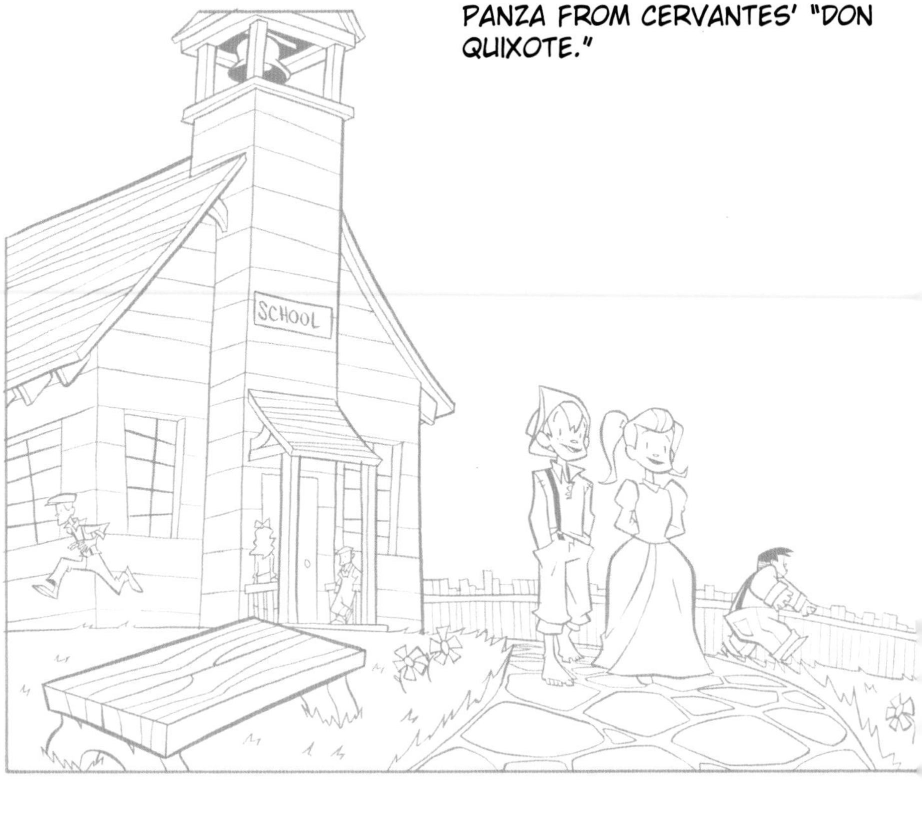
SCHOOL

TWAIN'S ORIGINAL INTENTIONS WERE TO HAVE TOM MATURE AND TRAVEL TO MANY LANDS THROUGHOUT THE PROGRESS OF THE FIRST NOVEL. WHILE TOM APPEARED IN "THE ADVENTURES OF HUCKLEBERRY FINN" (1884), IT WASN'T UNTIL MUCH LATER THAT HIS PLANS FOR HIS YOUNG ADVENTURER WERE REALIZED WHEN HE PUBLISHED "TOM SAWYER ABROAD" (1894) AND "TOM SAWYER, DETECTIVE" (1896). "TOM SAWYER ABROAD" SEES TOM, HUCK, AND JIM TRAPPED IN A RUNAWAY BALLOON WITH A MAD SCIENTIST, AND "TOM SAWYER, DETECTIVE" PLANTS THE BOYS BACK IN HANNIBAL, WHERE TOM ATTEMPTS TO SOLVE A MYSTERIOUS MURDER.

ONE OF THE KEY'S TO TWAIN'S POPULARITY WAS HIS ABILITY TO CAPTURE THE LIFESTYLE AND LANGUAGE OF THE COMMON, EVERYDAY PERSON. HE HAD A TRUE EAR FOR COLLOQUIAL SPEECH, AND THE ABILITY TO BRING THAT SPEECH, AND THE LIVES OF ITS SPEAKERS, TO THE WRITTEN PAGE.

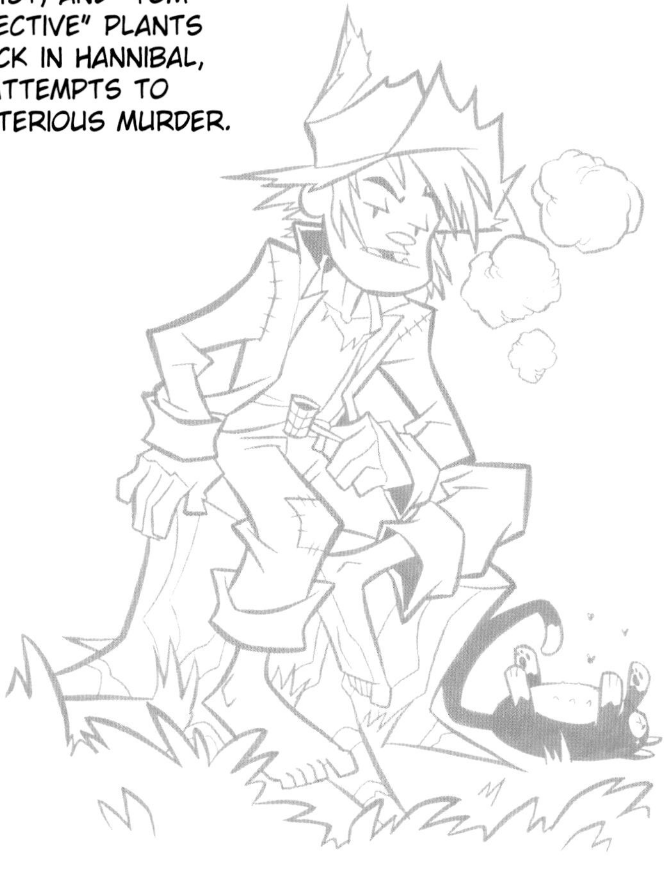

IN TWAIN'S TIME, EDUCATION WAS A LUXURY THAT MANY PEOPLE COULDN'T AFFORD. THE BUILDING OF SCHOOL HOUSES AND THE EMPLOYMENT OF TEACHERS WERE COMMUNITY EFFORTS, AND WHILE THE RUDIMENTARY EDUCATIONAL SYSTEM DEPENDED UPON THE COMMUNITY, THE COMMUNITY ALSO DEPENDED UPON THE EDUCATIONAL SYSTEM TO TEACH ITS CHILDREN THE PRACTICAL KNOWLEDGE THEY NEEDED.

CHILDREN WERE TAUGHT BY PURE MEMORIZATION, THE FORMAL CURRICULUM CENTERED AROUND SPELLING, READING, WRITING, AND ARITHMETIC, BUT MORE USEFUL SKILLS WERE TAUGHT AS WELL.

"I HAVE NEVER LET MY SCHOOLING GET IN THE WAY OF MY EDUCATION."

–MARK TWAIN

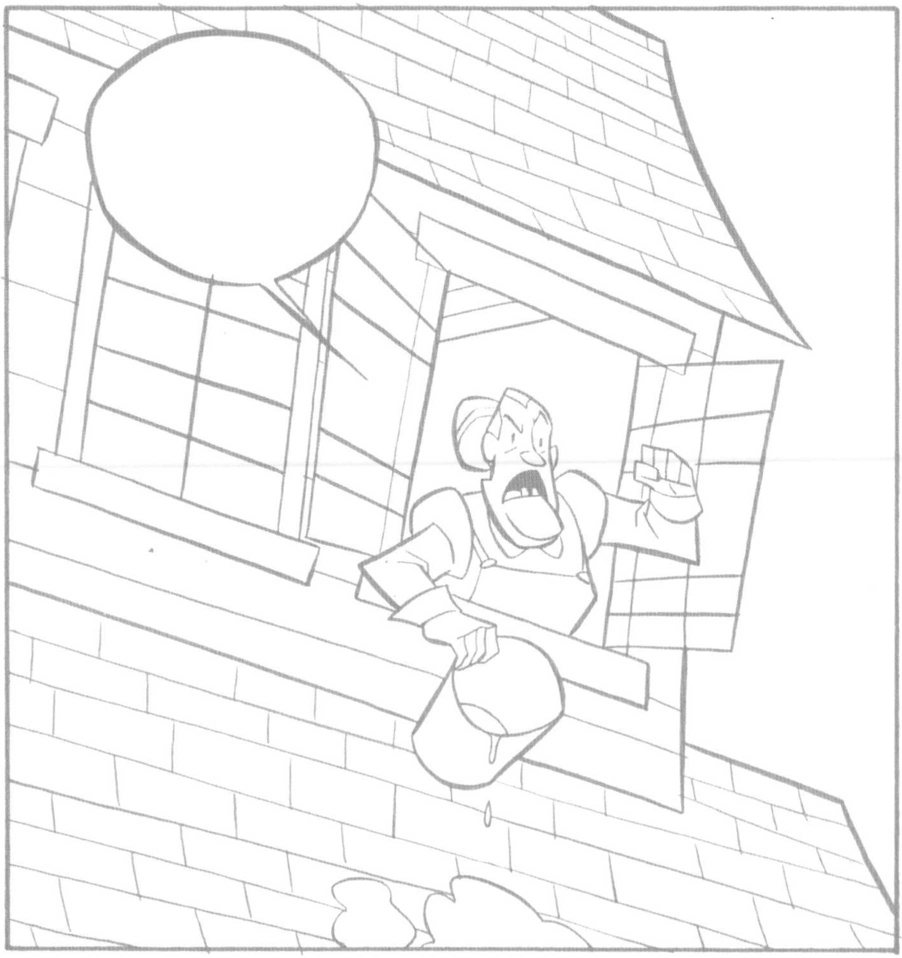

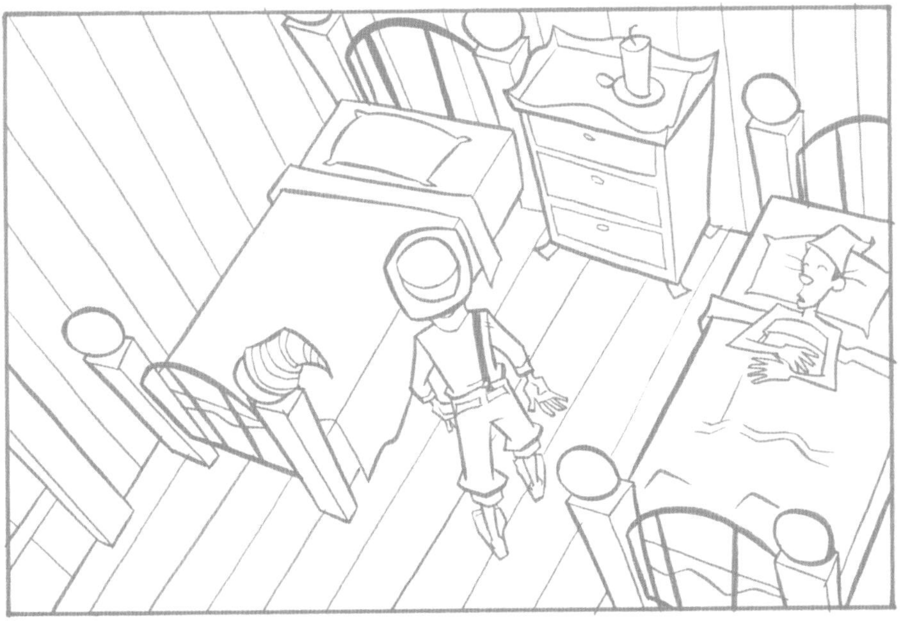

STUDENTS COULD BE EXPECTED TO LEARN HOW TO FARM, SEW, MEND CLOTHES, AND DO GENERAL HOUSEWORK, IN ADDITION TO THEIR PENMANSHIP LESSONS. TEXTBOOKS WERE SO RARE THAT MANY SCHOOLS TAUGHT FROM THE BIBLE, WHICH WAS A BOOK MANY FAMILIES OWNED, AND STUDENTS WOULD PRACTICE THEIR LESSONS ON A WRITING SLATE (LIKE A CHALK-BOARD), WHICH WAS CHEAPER AND MORE DURABLE THAN PAPER.

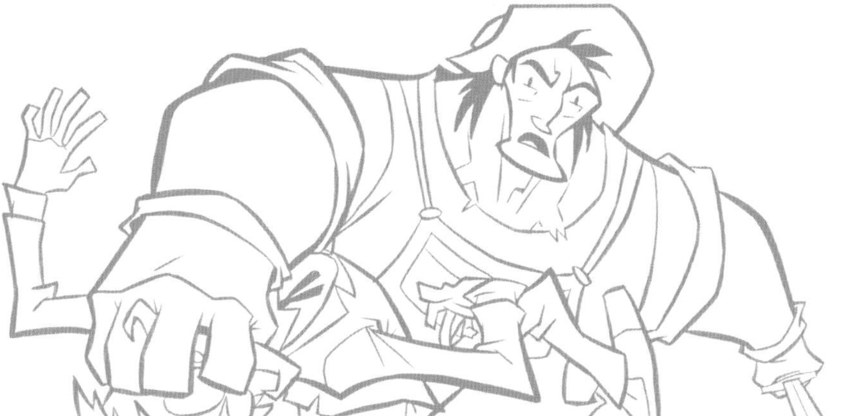

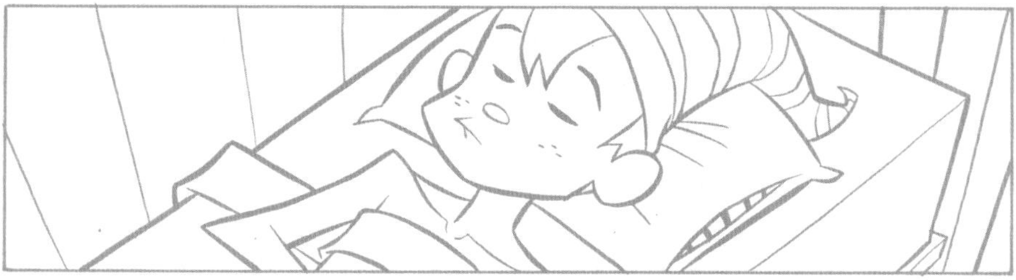

THROUGHOUT HIS LIFETIME TWAIN TRAVELED ALL OVER THE WORLD, OBSERVING AND LEARNING. TRAVEL IN HIS DAY WAS RELEGATED TO HORSE DRAWN COACHES, SHIPS AND BOATS, OR TRAINS. AIR TRAVEL WAS VERY RARE, AND THE AUTOMOBILE INDUSTRY WAS IN ITS INFANCY. RIVERS LIKE THE MISSISSIPI, WHICH TWAIN WORKED ON AS A RIVERBOAT PILOT, WERE IMMENSELY IMPORTANT TO THE NATION'S TRADE AND ECONOMY. IN A LETTER TO HIS CHILDHOOD FRIEND WILL BOWEN, TWAIN WROTE, "THE ONLY REAL, INDEPENDENT & GENUINE GENTLEMEN IN THE WORLD GO QUIETLY UP AND DOWN THE MISSISSIPPI RIVER, ASKING NO HOMAGE OF ANY ONE, SEEKING NO POPULARITY, NO NOTORIETY & NOT CARING A DAMN WHETHER SCHOOL KEEPS OR NOT." ON APRIL 21, 1910, SAM CLEMENS DIED AT THE AGE OF 74 AT HIS HOUSE IN REDDING, CONNECTICUT.

"RUMOURS OF MY DEATH HAVE BEEN GREATLY EXAGGERATED."

–MARK TWAIN

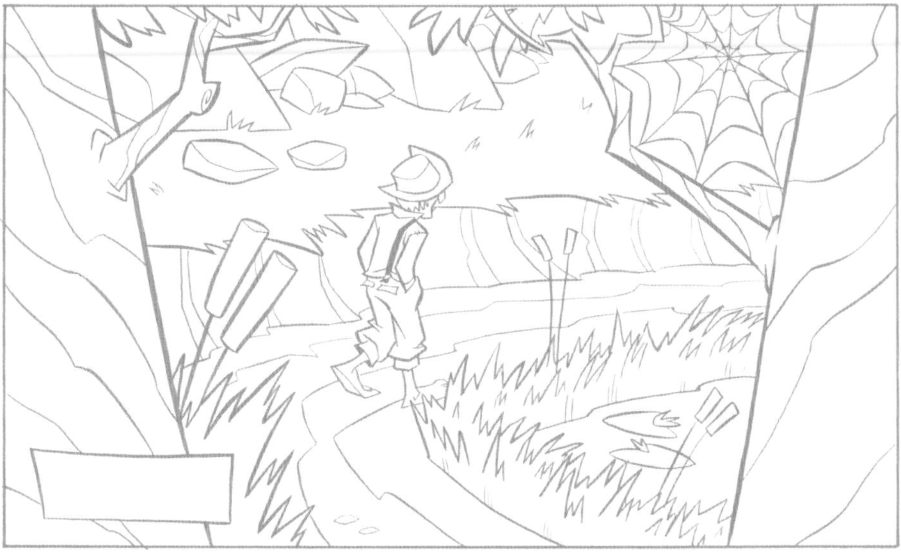

MARK TWAIN WROTE HUNDREDS OF BOOKS, ESSAYS, AND ARTICLES THROUGHOUT HIS LIFE. HERE ARE SOME OF HIS MORE FAMOUS WORKS. IN ADDITION TO "TOM SAWYER" AND OTHER ADVENTURE STORIES, TWAIN WAS ALSO INTERESTED IN POLITICAL REFORM AND CONTINUED TO TRAVEL AND WRITE ABOUT TRAVEL UNTIL HIS DEATH.

(1867) ADVICE FOR LITTLE GIRLS (FICTION)

(1867) THE CELEBRATED JUMPING FROG OF CALAVERAS COUNTY (STORIES)

(1869) THE INNOCENTS ABROAD (NONFICTION TRAVEL)

(1872) ROUGHING IT (NON-FICTION)

(1873) THE GILDED AGE: A TALE OF TODAY (FICTION)

(1875) SKETCHES NEW AND OLD (FICTIONAL STORIES)

(1876) OLD TIMES ON THE MISSISSIPPI (NONFICTION)

(1876) THE ADVENTURES OF TOM SAWYER (FICTION)

(1877) A TRUE STORY AND THE RECENT CARNIVAL OF CRIME (STORIES)

(1880) A TRAMP ABROAD (NONFICTION TRAVEL)

(1882) THE PRINCE AND THE PAUPER (FICTION)

(1883) LIFE ON THE MISSISSIPPI (NONFICTION)

(1884) ADVENTURES OF HUCKLEBERRY FINN (FICTION)

(1889) A CONNECTICUT YANKEE IN KING ARTHUR'S COURT (FICTION)

(1894) TOM SAWYER ABROAD (FICTION)

(1894) PUDD'N'HEAD WILSON (FICTION)

(1896) TOM SAWYER, DETECTIVE (FICTION)

(1897) FOLLOWING THE EQUATOR (NONFICTION TRAVEL)

(1901) EDMUND BURKE ON CROKER AND TAMMANY (POLITICAL SATIRE)

(1902) A DOUBLE BARRELLED DETECTIVE STORY (FICTION)

(1905) KING LEOPOLD'S SOLILOQUY (POLITICAL SATIRE)

(1906) THE $30,000 BEQUEST AND OTHER STORIES (FICTION)

(1935) MARK TWAIN'S NOTEBOOK (PUBLISHED POSTHUMOUSLY)